VALLEY OF DIAMONDS

VALLEY OF
DIAMONDS

Edward D. Smith

Order this book online at www.trafford.com
or email orders@trafford.com

Most Trafford titles are also available at major online book retailers.

Printed in the United States of America.

ISBN: 978-1-4669-0273-2 (sc)
ISBN: 978-1-4669-0274-9 (e)

Trafford rev. 11/11/2011

 www.trafford.com

North America & International
toll-free: 1 888 232 4444 (USA & Canada)
phone: 250 383 6864 ♦ fax: 812 355 4082

PROLOGUE

RORY ADAMS SAT at his desk in a tiny stifling office, deciding how to get his precious cargo to Yengema.

At 23 years old, he was six feet tall, lean and healthy. It was his first job after graduating from The Camborne School of Mines in Cornwall, England. Though he was a trained geologist, he had been working for two years, helping to run this small, productive diamond mine in Guinea, West Africa. When the previous manager had left a year ago, he took over. He supposed he should have prepared some kind of evacuation plan when the war in France started going wrong for the Allies, but he hadn't.

Rory was taken by surprise when he received a letter from the company office in Conakry, ordering him to close the mine and leave *immediately*. It had also said that he was to travel to Yengema in Sierra Leone *with any production and current records*. He liked their vague description.

It was late June, 1940 and he was leaving. His assistant, David Warner, had already left in the company-owned Ford. Rory decided they wouldn't be so conspicuous if they travelled separately and met again at the Kuku river ford. From there, they could travel to Yengema together. David had travelled to Yengema before and knew the route. Rory, however, had never been there.

David knew he should leave as soon as possible, but couldn't generate enough energy to move. He also had a premonition that something would happen to him on the journey, making him reluctant to start. The afternoon sun poured through the windows, baking every inch of the room. Though it was dry at the mine, there had been thunderstorms the night before and it had rained ten miles away. The office was very plainly furnished, with a few chairs, a safe, a few shelves and two tables. Due to his imminent departure, the office had not been swept properly for several days. The furniture and floor were covered with a thick layer of dust and sand, brought in on the soles of people's shoes, or the bare feet of the labourers. His office was joined to the clerk's office by a connecting doorway. Though he was only wearing shorts and a light shirt, he was soaked with sweat. He knew he needed to hurry. German troops were expected to arrive soon.

He had locked up the plant and the compound, leaving one set of keys with Abdul Kourouma, his clerk." When the war finishes I'll come back. Stay here, you'll be paid. Just try to save the plant from being destroyed. You've worked well for me and I'll tell them in London."

All the other keys were bundled together in his knapsack. He took the rough diamonds from his safe and emptied them from their containers onto his desk. They'd accumulated a total of 20,000 carats from the rich areas they'd been mining. Because of the fighting in France, they hadn't sent any out for weeks.

He divided the diamonds into two piles. The larger pile consisted of diamonds, each one less than five carats. These were placed in a canvas bag that he put in a small, metal biscuit tin. He put the larger diamonds into a silver whiskey flask that his sister had given him for his eighteenth birthday. The biscuit tin went into the knapsack and the whiskey flask went into a pocket of his khaki jacket. Now, he was ready. The knapsack contained clothes, mine returns and items for his journey. He placed his arms through the straps of his rucksack and slung it over his shoulders.

He went outside, said goodbye to Abdul and mounted his Brough Superior motorcycle. Abu, his houseboy, was travelling with him, but would leave just before they arrived at the Kulu River. Rory was sorry he was leaving a place where he'd been so happy, but at the same time he was looking forward to the trip. Glancing at his watch, he realized he should have left before. It would be difficult to arrive before dark. Still, he set out in good spirits, with Abu seated on the pillion seat behind him.

Though the roads near the mine were dry, the single road ten miles away through a patch of forest was wet and very difficult to pass. It had rained for several days and the road was soft and muddy. When the motorcycle got bogged down in the mud, Abu helped him push it to firmer ground and they carried on. Abu left him about a mile from the Kulu river.

"If you see Saa, tell him to look after the Brough. Change the oil and start up the engine occasionally."

"I will master. Take care on your journey. God be with you."

"You too, Abu! I'll see you again."

It had taken a long time to travel 60 miles, as the roads were in such a bad state. The country was also in a state of turmoil. There were a lot of armed bandits, mainly deserters from the army, who were robbing travelers on the roads. Rory and Abu left the road and hid in the forest every time they saw strangers. He felt sad and alone when Abu left him.

It was dark when Rory arrived at the end of the track to ford the Kulu river. The river was flowing swiftly and it was very high and wide. He put his motorcycle on its stand and dismounted. Stiff and sore from his journey, he was very tired and wanted to rest. He couldn't see David Warner, or his Ford, on the other side of the river. Saa, one of his drivers should have been waiting for him near the ford. Rory found it difficult to make up his mind. He didn't know whether to try to wade across the river by himself, or wait. He'd arranged for Saa to take the motorcycle back to the mine, but needed to find Warner who would take him to Yengema. Going into the nearby village to find Saa would be too dangerous. After thinking about it, he decided to wait for Warner and his motorcar. They could cross the river early the next day when the water was low.

Rory turned the motorcyle around, wheeled it under a tree and put it on its stand. The soil under the tree was soft and dry, so he decided to sleep there. But, he was also worried about sleeping with the flask of valuable diamonds near him. It was made of silver, attractive to a thief. He removed it from his pocket and looked around for a suitable place to hide it. He found a small hole, presumably made by some animal, under the roots of a large tree. He stuffed the flask into it and covered the entrance with moss and mud. He left a small knife with his initials, *RHA*, on it as a marker. He returned to his motorcycle to wait for Saa, or David Warner. He sat on the ground and leaned against the motorcycle.

While waiting, Rory thought about where he'd buried the diamonds and decided it was an unsafe hiding place. *The flask might be uncovered by water flowing down the path during the night,* he thought. He walked back to the hiding place, removed the moss and mud from the hole, removed the flask and then walked back up the road. He walked about 50 feet and found an untouched patch of forest. He looked for a tree he could easily recognize in the morning. There was a large stout tree, dividing into two thick stems six feet up. It reminded him of a similar tree in his parent's garden out in Chipping Warden. He buried the flask containing the diamonds into a small, rocky hole under the tree roots. Again, he filled the hole with soil and moss. He used a small branch, which he broke off from a small shrub, to mark the spot. He went back to the first hiding place to retrieve his knife, but couldn't find it. He walked back to his motorcycle and took a blanket out of his knapsack.

He didn't worry about the two large diamonds he'd concealed in the motorcycle behind the reflector of his headlight. He was sure that no one knew that he had hidden them there. He had been very clever and cunning in acquiring and hiding them. Originally, he had meant to remove them before he met David, but the weather and events had caused him to forget. He was now more concerned with his own safety and only wished to reach Sierra Leone alive. He hoped Saa would look after his Brough.

He spread out his blanket and folded it. He put the knapsack at the top, as a pillow. He lay down, pulled one half over him and went to sleep. Even though he blanket got damp from the water percolating through the foliage of the tree, he was exhausted and slept soundly. He awoke when he heard the sounds of someone walking along the path. "David?" he queried, trying to see who it was.

CHAPTER 1

HOWARD EVANS AWOKE. As usual, he stretched out his right arm to feel the warm, smooth body of his young wife. She was asleep, but his touch produced a warm smile. She was happy.

The large, carpeted bedroom smelled pleasantly of Jean's perfume. She was a petite woman of only 5' 1". When Howard had first seen her, he thought she looked like a delicate Dresden porcelain statuette. She had auburn hair and blue eyes. As he got to know her, he also came to understand how mentally tough and intelligent she was. The porcelain statue had a steel rod holding it together.

He had spent a disturbed night. Even though his police training had conditioned him to make quick decisions, this was different. His decision to accept employment in Guinea, West Africa, had caused him to have nighmares. He remembered dreaming of being chased around a forest by a gang of Africans, carrying spears.

But now, wide awake in his comfortable house in Banbury England, he realized this was an opportunity to recoup his financial losses. He had been offered a good job as a security officer on a diamond mine. *What could go wrong?* The fact that the company wanted him out there within two weeks worried him. The two weeks had disappeared and he was going the next day. He now realized what he was giving up.

They lived in the upper part of the town, near the hospital. After breakfast, they walked along the rural path, lined with hedgerows on top of the hill, down the road to Broad Street. Solid old houses lined the roads. One evening, he'd seen a fox walking doglike long the path, blending in with the people and the dogs. As usual, on Saturdays, the town was full of people because of the market that was held in the old square near the Town Hall. They walked there. The butcher's store had a line in front of it. They were famous for their good quality, inexpensive meat. The fruit and vegetable store had fresh produce from the market gardens in the Vale of Evesham. Jean spoke to the owner for a long time. As she was one of the owner's many relatives, she was given special attention. It was one of those autumn days when everything went well for him. The weather was perfect, it was a warm sunny day, and they had a pleasant, inexpensive lunch in the Woolpack.

After lunch they continued their walk around the town. They went for a drink at Ye Olde Reindeer Inn on Parsons Street. The bar was crowded, so they didn't spend much time there. Afterwards, on the way home, they went to look at the famous Banbury Cross.

In the evening, some of his police friends arranged a party at the White Lion. He enjoyed being with them, though he knew most of them thought he was mad to leave his wife and go off to a place like Guinea.

The next day, even though he didn't want to leave England, he went to Guinea.

CHAPTER 2

*H*OWARD'S PROBLEMS HAD started some time before when his friend David Rhys had retired after 30 years with the Banbury police. David had asked Howard if he would like to be his partner in an inquiry agency he was starting. Howard liked being a police officer and knew he had a good chance of promotion because his reports by senior officers were always favourable.

On impulse, he'd resigned and invested his life's savings in the business.

He'd liked the idea of being a partner and working in a business with his friend. After three months, though, sitting around the office with little to do, he realized there wasn't enough business to support the two of them. They also didn't have enough capital to sustain themselves until the business picked up. They weren't getting too many inquiries regarding detective work and the security jobs, or protection business at night didn't pay enough. Howard realized he had done a very stupid thing and jepardized his family's future. His friends advised him to rejoin the police force. Rhys offered to sell the agency to Howard for a nominal amount. But he couldn't take advantage of his friend. He also hated to admit that he'd made a mistake and dreaded the ribbing he knew he'd get from his friends in the police force. Instead, he decided to get another job and work for someone else until he had enough money to make a success of his inquiry agency. Even Jean thought he was being stubborn, though she didn't harp on it. She liked his spirit of independence, giving up his solid job to start a business.

When one of his police friends mentioned that there was a vacancy for a security officer in Guinea, he'd applied for the job. DIASA's main office was a large Victorian mansion on the xford Road in Banbury. He knew little about Guinea, except that it was in West Africa and presumably very hot. So, he checked out some books from the public library and read what he could about it. He wasn't too impressed. The president there appeared to have communist ideas and was a dictator who liked to watch people being tortured; a sort of latter day Nero. When Richard Compton interviewed him in the Banbury office of DIASA, however, he'd made Guinea sound as though it was a tropical paradise in the making. Still, Howard noticed that not too many projects on the diamond mine seemed to be finished, though they were being built.

"We've finished about 30 houses. The club is almost finished and the hospital is in the planning stage. Also, we now have a plane, so we don't have the ten hour road trip from Conakry," Richard explained.

Howard could tell that Richard wanted him to take the job. The salary offered was very generous, though Richard mentioned, "Other applicants."

Afterwards, they went and had lunch in the White Lion Hotel.

A few days later, when Howard was offered the job, he began to have doubts about the wisdom of accepting it. His friends in the police force then told him that a former policeman named Mark Buzzard worked there. He'd heard of Buzzard's unsavoury reputation, causing him to have doubts more about the calibre of the people working on the mine. Still, he decided to be adventurous, travel to Guinea and see what it was like to work under the unusual conditions. He knew Jean had always thought he was too cautious and he wanted to change her opinion. So, he accepted the job.

Jean helped him to pack a large suitcase to take with him. They travelled down to Heathrow, with her brother, to catch an evening flight to Paris. Howard nearly changed his mind about going when he left them at Heathrow, but he knew he couldn't face the derision he would receive from his friends.

After a comfortable night in a hotel near Charles de Gaulle Airport, he felt happier and was ready for his adventure. On the tedious flight from Paris to Conakry, however, he again changed his mind and realized he was giving up too much. As the plane got nearer to the equator, it got hotter and and stuffier in the crowded cabin. He grew more uneasy. To take his mind off his uncomfortably cramped seat, he looked out of the plane's window and watched the landscape below. It had changed from the orderly settled areas of Europe to the scattered villages amid the sand dunes of the Sahara desert. There were huge shadows near the dunes, air near the ground shimmering in the heat. He'd never been outside Europe before and didn't realize conditions would be so different in Africa. He didn't know if he could adapt to such a different lifestyle and thought he should have stayed in England. When the plane swooped low over Conakry and he saw its lush vegetation and bustling streets, though, he became a little happier.

As the only passenger who was going to the mine at Matakourou, he was met at the airport by a Guinean driver wearing a hat inscribed *DIASA*. Without delay, formalities were quickly exchanged and he was on the dual carriage way to the Independence Hotel. The mini bus was a new Volkswagen.

The hotel was run like a French hotel. The rooms were large and air-conditioned, and the meals were of the highest quality. His large bedroom was air-conditioned with a television set. However, he was disappointed with the programmes. He had dinner in the hotel and spent a comfortable night in his air-conditioned bedroom. His stay at the Independence allayed his fears about the standard of his future accommodations in Guinea.

The air trip from Conakry to Matakourou in the company Cessna also impressed him. The plane looked new, while the pilot and co-pilot were dressed in clean, pressed uniforms. He was met at the airport by his boss, Sean MacVeigh, and his wife, Maureen. They were in a new Range Rover. Sean was 50 years old, very sun-tanned, six feet tall, with a quiet Southern Irish accent. He was wearing khaki slacks and shirt, almost a uniform. His wife, Maureen, seemed much younger. She was very slim and had an English accent that Howard had known as a county accent. She was wearing a cream skirt and white shirt, and Howard caught the hint of an expensive perfume. The road to the houses was tarred. Lunch at their house on the hill confirmed that life here could be very comfortable. The house was large and made of some concrete material. It was air-conditioned, with heavy, well-made furniture. Lunch was served in a small dining room and a uniformed African waited on them. It reminded Howard of a scene in a Somerset Maughan novel.

When he arrived at Banam along a terrible road in a Landrover, he knew that his fears were well founded. The road meandered across the countryside, with very few straight stretches. It had rained the previous night and the road was wet. In places, it was haphazardly gravelled. In others, it consisted mainly of mud. Just before the camp, they drove through a river that had a pebbled bottom. Then, they passed through a small patch of forest along a rutted road into the camp. The driver stopped outside a small container-like structure. It looked out of place in this rural setting. Howard helped the driver unload the luggage and went inside. He heard the Landrover drive away. Sitting on the large bed inside the crowded cabin, he wondered about the people who would work in such conditions.

People like Sean had worked in Africa for years. Others like him were trying to make and save money as quickly as possible. Some people would find it difficult to obtain a job in England. The senior mangement in England, most of whom had worked in mining all their lives, held the organization together.

CHAPTER 3

*H*OWARD EVANS AWOKE ans stretched out his right arm, expecting to feel the warm, smooth body of his young wife. It was as though he needed physical proof that the person he loved most in life was still close to him.

Other people he'd cared about had died, or left him. His mother had died when he was young. Afterwrds, his father didn't seem to know how to provide a home for him. He'd lived with his grandmother who had been like a mother to him. Her death, two years ago, had left an aching void in his life and his loneliness lasted until he met Jean.

His arm reached out into nothingness. Instead of the silky smoothness of her skin and the regular, rhythmic movements of her body, he felt the rough, inhuman texture of the sweaty sheets. There was a pungent smell of the coarse soap used in washing bed linen. Jean wasn't there. She was in England and he was here in Guinea, West Africa. For a moment, still half asleep, he was confused and couldn't understand where he was. The mixture of odours, dampness, disinfectant from the toilet, cooking smells from yesterday's meals and the pungent smell of scorched insects soon brought him back to reality. His solitary state saddened him, but he soon recovered.

The darkness was retreating. It got light quickly here and the electric outside the main door was on because the generator had been started. The loud, throbbing, metalic noise had awoken him. He could also hear the buzzing of insects attracted to the light. Howard knew he didn't belong here. He should be with his wife in Banbury, especially since she was pregnant with their first child. He slowly opened his eyes. On the opposite wall was a token of her love. Hanging on the wall was the needlepoint tapestry of Banbury Cross that she had made for him and slipped into his suitcase. He looked up at the white lined ceiling and paused for a few moments, Letting his eyes roam the crowded room. It was very clean and well organized. The arrangement was more utilitarian than cozy and it lacked style. It was as if the designer drew a plan considerate of what he could fit inside the space, while someone went out and bought the items as cheaply as possible. It reminded him of a cabin he had once occupied on a cheap cruise ship in the Meditterean. He was living in a steel box, a converted container, like the type used to transport goods on ships. There were three areas. The bedroom contained a large bed, much too large for the space, with a set of drawers for his clothes, and a wardrobe. The unmarried men got a smaller bed that made the cabin more comfortable. It was divided from the living room and kitchen by a sliding plastic screen. It was cramped and very hot inside. The Canadian Chief Executive Officer, Alec MacIntyre, had seen these conversions at a trade show and realized how useful they would be on the mine. They were self-contained and came out from England with all the necessary furniture, utensils, electrical connections and plumbing. There was a large galvanized steel water storage tank on the roof that was kept full of water piped from springs up the hill.

Even though he was naked, he was sweating from the heat. The bedroom had a built in air-conditioning unit, but it was electric and had only just been switched on. At Banam, the electric generator was normally shut down at midnight. He glanced through the open venetian blinds that covered one of the windows. The early morning sunlight was streaming through and he could see particles of dust floating on its rays. He sat up, lifted back the single sheet on top of him, swivelled on his hips and planted his feet firmly on the tufted rug. He was wide awake now and ready for his Saturday morning patrol around the mine. He pulled back the screen and walked into the kitchen area.

He filled the kettle with water from the ceramic filter and boiled it on the gas stove. The gas came from a bottle outside the trailer. A tea bag in a mug filled with the boiling water provided a hot drink. After removing the tea bag and throwing it in the plastic waste bin, he drank some of the tea. He left the mug on the counter and walked into the shower. There was a small room on the side that also contained a flush toilet. After showering, he returned to the main room, dried himself with a towel and changed into his shorts and shirt. He shaved in the large sink that had a mirror above it. When he had finished, he examined his face for signs of aging. He always thought his face was too youthful. For all of his 25 years, he'd always wanted to look more rugged. Looking at his refection reminded him of his wife, so he sat down at the table and gazed at her photograph. He also had a larger photograph taken with him, hanging on the wall. He thought how lucky he was to have found such a perfect companion.

Breakfast consisted of cornflakes, milk and another cup of tea. As it was Saturday, he found his bottle of anti malaria tablets and took one. He wasn't used to taking pills regularly and found it irksome. The doctor in England had emphasized how important it was not to get malaria. He put the food back, washed up the crockery and returned it to its cupboard.

He decided to do some physical exercise outside. He was still amazed at how bright the sunlight was, even this early in the morning. He stepped down from his trailer onto a bamboo mat that was under a straw shaded annex. He did a series of stretching exercises, followed by a series of push-ups. After his exercises, he felt more calm. He stood and looked down the valley to the hills near the main camp at Matakourou. The small camp at Banam was laid out along the valley and up the hill on one side. He looked along the road and could see the houses along his road, laid out like the benches in a Roman ampitheatre. Below were the offices, other buildings and the club. The roads and building destroyed the serenity of this small, verdant valley with its bubbling stream at the bottom. Still, it was very beautiful.

He'd only been here two weeks, so he still wasn't used to living in such a primitive fashion. He could see why the previous Security man had resigned after only a year. This was his first job in West Africa. If he didn't need the money so badly, he would have also resigned when he saw the conditions. But today was cooler than it had been for several days and he was getting used to the conditions. Though he missed Jean, he felt happy.

His Landrover was parked at the side of the building on a small, bulldozed hill. The company did it because it saved having to replace expensive starters. But his Security Landrover did have a starter. So, he went there to start his patrol. The keys were still in it. He thought it a little irresponsible until he remembered where he was. *Who would steal a Landrover in this part of Guinea?* The authorities would catch anyone within hours. His job today was to drive around the Banan valley to see if there were any illegal diggers in the DIASA lease area. So far, he had not seen any illegals. The government had promised the company they would prevent the type of diggings seen in places like Sierra Leone. So far, they'd kept their promise.

Howard switched the vehicle on, pushed down on the clutch pedal and ran it down the hill onto the road when it started. The hillside above the houses was clothed with tall grass and fire-scorched shrubs and trees. At one time, it had been used for grazing cattle. The local people torched it annually to get rid of the snakes and to encourage a more vigorous growth of grass after the longer spring rains. He hadn't seen any snakes, but he had been told there were a lot of gaboon vipers on the hill.

It was just before 7:00 am, so he decided to start his patrol at the far mining cut. This was five miles away, along a damp and rapidly drying road. There had been a small shower during the night.

He passed the new village, with its thatched mud houses where the Guinean labourers lived. A group of women, dressed in colourful clothes and carrying laundry, wished him, "Good morning." They did have piped water in the village from standpipes, but most of them preferred to do their washing in the traditional way on rocks in the stream. He felt sorry for the young girls following the older women. They had tall, galvanised buckets on their heads that looked too large for their small bodies. Often, he noticed them kneeling in the river, scooping up water into their buckets with calabashes. Clearly, they weren't strong enough to lift full buckets onto their heads. He always thought they looked undernourished and didn't wear enough clothes. This was particularly true when it rained and they got soaked. They only had cheap cotton clothes that weren't waterproof. He didn't like the idea of living in a country where people were so poor, but he also knew he could do very little to help. Still he decided he would try his best to help them.

He noticed one woman in the group carrying some of his clothes. Jean had bought him a distinctive pair of pants in the Littlewoods store in Banbury that had chocolate ribs, with a pattern of small flowers. Though he knew no one would see them. He'd avoided wearing them in England because he thought they were too gaudy. When he noticed that Jean had packed them in his luggage, he wore them because they reminded him of her. As a newcomer to Africa, he was fascinated by the ease with which the women carried their laundry in buckets on their heads. He knew now they had a small ring made of grass under the buckets. Jeanine Kourouma organized the laundry collection and paid the laundresses from money supplied by the Camp Supervisor, Jeffrey Ellis. She also organized the house cleaning for the people who wanted it. Howard had his house cleaned every Monday. Jeanine assured him that he wouldn't have anything stolen. She'd added that the only things they'd ever lost from the laundry were women's underclothes. Apparantly, the laundry women couldn't get the same type of attractive underclothes as the ones which came from Europe. When some of the expatriate women heard about this, they solved the problem by donating some of their own. When on leave in England, they simply bought extras to give to the laundry women.

He carried on until he reached the current mine cut. The cut had only just been started. There were only two rows of overburden stacks, like miniature Alps, lined up in military columns at one side of the cut. The small dragline, standing at the end of the cut like some ominous bird of prey, was throwing its bucket forward to retrieve the gravel on the cut bed. The operator pulled a lever that brought the gravel in the bucket toward him and up to the top of the cut just below his machine. The gravel was stacked on the unmined side of the cut. Howard parked his Landrover at the top of the cut near the dewatering pumps. A Guinean homologue, a mining engineer, was supervising the mining. Howard walked over to him. The man greeted him with a curt, "Bonjour, Howard."

"Bonjour, Henri," Howard replied, "Ca va?"

"Bien," Henri replied.

Howard realized the man was stuck here all day in the hot sun, as he didn't have his own transport. He thought of offering him a lift to the plant, but decided against it. He wasn't sure how he was supposed to treat the homologues. He knew they didn't work directly for the company but for the Guinea government and weren't paid very much money. The man and his wife lived in one of the adobe houses in the old village.

Howard walked to the edge of the cut and looked down to the desiccated granite bedrock ten feet below. He was fascinated by the colours: red, green and blue among others. Afterwards, he watched a front end loader fill small dump trucks from the gravel stacks. The way the machine advanced to the truck, elevated the bucket, tipped and retreated back to the gravel pile reminded him of a praying mantis he had seen on the window sill in his little cabin. After watching the process for half an hour, he decided to move on. The thumping sound of the gravel as it fell from the bucket into the truck bodies gave him a headache. The trucks shuddered with the piledriver-like impact, but the drivers didn't appear to be affected by the noise or movement. The resulting dust cloud enveloped the whole area. He could feel a choking sensation in his throat when it passed through his nose into his lungs. This nearly caused him to be physically sick. He was surprised to see the dust, but realized the gravel was dry in the middle of the stacks. He didn't want to remain in such an unhealthy place, so he decided to visit the portable heavy media plant a mile away.

When one of the trucks was full, he followed it to the plant. The plant was built into the side of a hill 200 feet from the banks of the Kulu river. The top of the hill consisted of a large, flat area with a loading bay made of steel sheets overlooking the side of the hill. The small truck reversed and tipped its load into the bay. Howard drove down the road to the office at the bottom of the cut and parked near the Plant Engineer's Landrover.

The previous Security Officer had kept files of everyone who had anything to do with DIASA. Howard read the files and was amazed at the mount of information the man had collected. He knew Dan Spring had lived and worked in Banbury before he came here. That's where DIASA's main office was located. Spring had been recruited by the Personnel Manger because he was a very good plant fitter. He had been trained to run this plant by the former Plant Engineer, Claude Beer, who would run the main plant now being built in Matakourou. Howard walked into the office. Dan was seated inside, reading a magazine. He was a short, 5'7" stocky man about 25 years old. His swarthy complexion and jet black hair hinted that his forebears had come from a warmer climate than Britain.

"Morning, Dan," Howard said. "If you don't mind, I'd like to find out a little more about how the plant works. You're not too busy or doing repairs, or something like that?"

"No. I haven't got a Guinean Plant engineer today, but the two Security men are here. They're checking seal numbers in the concentrate store. Each expatriate has to have a Guinean with him. They're known as homologues and we're supposed to be training them to eventually take over our jobs. But most of them don't like it here and find excuses to go back to Conakry, as often as possible. They're in a worse position than we are because they don't get paid as much as us. We have enough cans for a diamond shipment to Matakourou next week. They'll tell us when they want them."

Mark Buzzard and his Guinean counterpart, Abdul Kouruma, walked into the office. Years earlier Howard had heard of Buzzard when he was in the Thames Valley Police Force. Buzzard had been a policeman who had the reputation of being unnecessarily brutal when arresting criminals. Eventually, he had been forced to resign after 20 years with the police. He was tall, the same six feet two as Howard, but heavy drinking and lack of exercise had destroyed his former muscular build. Now, he was just a fat and old 45 year old. His wife had divorced him ten years ago.

Abdul Kouruma was six feet tall and looked like the ex-military officer he was. He was dressed in very well pressed, khaki clothes. He was dark skinned, lean, athletic and had a hawk-like nose. He was 40 years old.

The two security men said, "Good morning," and left the office.

"The plant is running well today. We've had no problems so far. But let's start at the loading bay and work our way down."

"Sounds okay to me," Howard said.

They climbed up the steps to the loading bay. There was another ladder leading up to a catwalk above the loading bay. "Do you feel like climbing up there?"

"Yes. I may as well see the whole operation."

They climbed up to the ladder. In the middle of the catwalk, a Guinean was operating a firehose and directing the water onto the gravel in the loading bay below. The gravel was disappearing through steel bars into an outlet chute below.

"It's done like this, so the worker washing isn't near the gravel."

"All this climbing must keep you fit," Howard said.

"When things are going well, there's not too much walking," Dan replied, smiling.

"But let's show you what happens. The gravel is washed from here into vibrating, sizing trommels. This removes the large sizes and slimes. The water comes from the river and the slimes are pumped away from it. The large sizes go by conveyor over there." He pointed in the direction of a growing hill of large stones. "Not very pretty, is it?"

"I suppose it's necessary?" Howard replied.

"The main elements of the system are the centrifuge. The cone over there and the electric magnet below here retrieves the separation material. The material consists of ferro-silicon that sticks to the magnet. The centrifuge divides the light gravel and concentrate. Again, the light gravel is discarded and the concentrate goes into the closed bin with the spout. The concentrate is tapped off into milk churns every day and later it is sent to Matakourou to be sorted. That's when the diamonds are recovered. Now, let's go and see the rest of the operation." They climbed down the ladder to where a Guinean was standing under a roofed area.

"It all seems very simple."

"Well, basically it is, if people pay attention to the gauges and check everything is working properly. Shabani, here, has been working for mining companies for years and is very good." Howard shook Shabani's hand, and he and Dan went into the small office.

"Let's tell you a little more about this plant. I think the company is trying to mine out some of the rich areas to get money to build the main plant in Matakourou. The diamonds there are more equally distributed. You noticed the central section is on wheels. That's because this plant will be moved to another location when we've mined out this area. The diamonds are scattered and in sort of pockets, so we'll have to keep moving. All the vulnerable sections where we could lose diamonds are closed in with expanded metal screens. They each have two clasp locks. I have the key to one and the security man has a key to the other one. Which means unless there is collusion between at least two people, it's a secure system. Also, now we have the two homologues as added security. I don't think the Guinea government trusts foreigners too much."

"Are you going to the party at Matakourou tonight?" Howard asked, not liking the tone of the conversation.

"I'll say. There's not too much entertainment around here. I'm hoping things will improve and we can go to Matakourou more often now that the Rest Houses have been finished. I don't think I would have come here, if I'd realized how dull it can be. Though, I must say the money's good."

"Yes. I was hoping Jean could come out here later on. But, it's much too remote for a woman expecting a child."

"Is it your first?"

"Yes. We've only been married just over a year. I only knew she was pregnant after I'd accepted the job. Jean didn't want me to know, but one of my friend's wife congratulated me at my going away party and she had to tell me. I was in the Thames Valley Police, but resigned to start an Inquiry agency with a friend. Unfortunately, the business couldn't support two partners. I was very pleased when Richard Compton offered me this job and he seemed happy to take me on."

"Yes. The company was in a bit of a bind when George Smith resigned. Richard must have jumped with joy when he heard about you. They find it difficult to fill some of the jobs. But, I must say, they've found some good people."

"Thanks. I must go now. I have to check out the radio on signal hill in Banam."

"I'll see you at the party tonight. It should be fun."

"Okay. Thanks for the tour. I'm looking forward to the trip to Matakourou."

CHAPTER 4

*J*UST BEFORE ELEVEN o' clock, Howard started on his journey back to the camp. He had reached the labourers village when he noticed a figure striding toward him. Jeanine Kourouma was out jogging. She was wearing pink shorts, a yellow tee shirt and athelic shoes. Howard noticed the striking, slim, petite, blonde, French woman walking around the camp, but had not had a conversation with her. She was Abdul Kourouma's wife. She did not stop, continuing down the road toward the mobile plant He slowed down. As she passed him, he watched her reflection in his side mirror. He admired her trim figure and noticed the tensing and relaxing of the muscles in her legs as she ran along. Her blonde pony tail streamed out behind her, swishing and glinting in the sunlight like gold dust floating down a riffle. Behind her she left a whiff of some delicate perfume.

When he arrived back at the camp, he went to the small Security building that he shared with Abdul and a radio operator who had a separate office. He parked the Landrover and went inside. The Security compound just outside the labourers village wasn't finished, but eventually it was to contain offices, stores and houses for the Security personnel.

"Any messages, Tamba?' he asked. Suddenly, he remembered he should have checked before he went out this morning. He was still getting used to his new job as the Field Security Officer, Banam and the changed circumstances of working in West Africa.

"No. It's been very quiet today."

"Okay. Just keep the radio on until we come back from Matakourou tomorrow night. I'll take a portable radio. Saa Kisii will relieve you and I'll pay you a bonus."

Howard knew the best thing he could do for Tamba was to give him some dollars. He could use this to buy food and things like radios. This was illegal, but the local currency was not half as valuable so the company turned a blind eye to the practice.

"Yes Sir. No problem."

"Good man. I'm going up the hill to test the radio now." This was done every day but normally by a Guinean security man. But he did have a key.

He walked out of the office and took the road up the steep hill to the radio post and aerial overlooking the camp. The road was very steep and the rutted laterite surface curved in S shapes around the camp side of the hill. The vegetation near the top of the hill had been burned recently so it consisted mainly of shrubs, tall grass and flowers.

The walk up the hill took ten minutes, but even though he was very fit he was sweating when he arrived at the top. Some of the red dust he had kicked up stuck to his face. The top had been levelled to accommodate a small steel container that had a mast, guyed with steel cables towering over it. He paused for a few minutes to recover his breath, mop his face with his hankerchief and take in the view. It was breathtaking. It was a lovely cloudless day, a light breeze cooled him off and he could vaguely see Matakourou in the distance. There was an unusual, isolated, flat hill some miles to his left side. This had clumps of shrubs covering its steep, sloping sides. On top, there was a flat area, like a cricket pitch of several hundred square feet. He decided he must climb to the top of Table Top hill one day.

Howard was struck by how green and empty the country was toward Matakourou. There were just a small hill, the river and rolling plains. He couldn't even see any villages or other habitations.

He cut his musings short, unlocked the padlock on the door, opened the door and waited a few minutes. As though from a blast furnace, the stored heat from inside hit him. He took off his shirt and hung it over the open door, and then he went inside. There was a radio on a steel shelf welded to the walls. He switched on the radio set, pressed the *SEND* key and spoke.

"Banam, here, Howard Evans, any messages?" He was hesitant because he wasn't used to speaking on the radio.

"Matakourou, here. We're expecting you this evening. We can accommodate anyone because the Rest Houses are finished."

"Message received. We'll be there. See you tonight. Out" He switched off the radio and picked up his shirt, but decided not to put it on. He locked the door and descended the hill.

When he reached the bottom, he decided to speak to Bob Taylor, the acting Manager. At fifty Bob was a construction ex-General Foreman. His wife, Angeline, was living in the camp. They had two children at school in England. Howard liked the couple but found them to be rather cautious in making friends.

The door of the office was open, so he went inside. A massive man of 6'2" tall, Bob was sitting at his desk, writing. His huge, bricklayer's hand, enveloped the biro. But his writing was very neat and controlled.

"Morning, Howard. Everything Okay."

"Yes. We don't seem to have any problems. I just want to find out about transport for Matakourou this afternoon?"

"I shan't be able to go. I've got to finish these reports for Banbury. Alec MacIntyre is staying for the club opening and Richard Compton will take them back with him. But I'd like Angeline to go. The trip will do her good. It's a bit lonely for a woman in a place like Banam."

"Yes. I'll be pleased to look after her. How many vehicles are going?"

"We'll see at lunchtime. As long as we have one Landrover left here the rest can go. If anything happens we always have the radio to Matakourou."

"Okay. I'll see you at lunch then. The radio will be manned until we come back."

"Okay." Bob carried on writing. "Just one thing. Keep an eye on Mark Buzzard. He gets a bit stupid when he's had a few drinks. Angeline doesn't like him."

"Yes. I'll keep an eye on him. He was well-known in the Banbury police as a heavy drinker."

Recalling her birthday party the previous night, he knew there was tension between she and Buzzard. He also sensed she didn't wish her husband to know something Buzzard knew about her.

Buzzard had asked Mrs. Taylor, "Didn't your mother live in Witney for a number of years, Mrs. Taylor?"

The question seemed innocent, but Angeline visibly aged and looked near to tears. But she recovered. "Yes, we did live there for some years," Angeline replied in a soft, worried voice. Then, she hurried away into the house.

Buzzard chuckled. "Her mother was quite a well known hippie when she was young. She was into everything, drugs and sex. She was known as the merry widow. You know the type of person," he said to Howard.

Howard hadn't replied, but this exchange confirmed his low opinion of Buzzard. Howard walked back to his cabin, packed a small bag for the trip and returned to the club annex. This was a round building made of soil and concrete blocks, twenty feet in diameter. Above the three foot wall, there was a straw thatched roof supported by roughly cut poles. The concrete floor was covered with large reed mats. The building had been built using a hand machine to make the blocks, furnished simply with tables and chairs. Some of the chairs were of the fold up type, with canvas backs and seats.

The main building, which was used when the weather was bad, was made of concrete blocks with an aluminium sheeted roof. There was a kitchen, storehouse and a dining room with bar. The only television set was in the dining room. Normally, news episode tapes and VCR film tapes were played when they arrived from England. There was a serving hatch between the bar and the annex.

The annex waiter came out of the kitchen and greeted Howard. "What would you like, Mr. Evans?"

"Just a Stella beer, Saa. Thank you."

The man went inside and came back with a frosted tankard filled with beer.

"Oh, that's great." He went and sat in one of the canvas chairs, enjoying a rest and quaffing his cold beer.

Tom Gough, the Prospecting supervisor, Tom Gough, who ran the sampling plant came in, looking very hot and sweating profusely. The waiter brought him a beer without being asked.

"Thanks, Saa. You knew what I needed. It's hot today."

The overweight, out of condition man slumped into a chair.

"I'm getting too old for these hot countries," he said, breathing heavily. "The doctor has told me not to drink. But what does he expect me to do?"

"Yes, I find it debilitating after England." "You'll get used to it after awhile."

Jeffrey Ellis, the Camp Supervisor, came in from the kitchen. He was a young, fit man of medium height who supervised the running of the camp. He was an ex-army cook who ran the kitchen and the camp with military precision. Howard didn't like his obsequious manner toward the people senior to him, or his bullying manner to those junior to him. Still, the Guineans appeared to like working for him.

People started coming into the annex and Ellis announced, "Lunch is ready in the dining room, if anyone wants it."

Howard went into the dining room where a curry lunch was laid out on a large table. People helped themselves and then carried it back to another table. Jeanine Kourouma came in to speak to Jeffrey Ellis. "Do you mind if I have lunch here," she asked, "Abdul has gone to visit some of his friends."

"Of course, you can. We'd like to see you here more often."

She sat at Howard's table and went to get some of the curry. Howard saw Buzzard at the curry table. "Don't do that," he heard Jeanine say, but could not see what had happened.

"That man's an animal," she said when she brought her meal back to Howard's table.

"What happened?" Howard asked.

"He squeezed my shoulder, shall we say. He apologized and said he was only being friendly."

"Would you like me to talk to him?"

"No. It's a waste of time. A lot of men think because I'm married to an African I must be promiscuous. They don't realize I love Abdul."

"I'm sorry."

"You get used to it."

"Are you going to the party in Matakourou?" Howard asked.

"I haven't thought about it, but would like to come."

"Would Abdul agree?"

"He won't be back till tomorrow evening."

"You can come as long as it won't cause trouble for you."

"Abdul knows he can trust me and doesn't worry about me anymore. He's upset because we haven't had children."

Jeffrey Ellis came into the room with glasses and some bottles of red wine. "Would you like some wine. Mrs. Kourouma? It's Beaujolais."

"Yes, thanks Jeffrey."

Jeffrey poured out a glass for Jeanine. "A votre sante, Madame."

"Merci, Monsieur."

Howard got himself a glass of wine.

Bob and Angeline Taylor came in and sat down at one of the empty tables. The waiter brought Bob a beer and Angeline a glass of wine. After a few minutes, he rapped the table with a spoon to gain attention. "Who wants to go to the party tonight?" he asked.

"I want to go and Jeanine here would like to go," Howard said.

"I'd like to go," Dan Spring said.

"I can stay with my friend, Fred. So, I'd like to go," Mark Buzzard said.

"Okay. We'll send three Landrovers. Dan, you take the Prospecting Landrover. You don't need it do you, Tom?"

"No. It's too humid for me today."

"Howard, I'd like you to take Jeanine in your Landrover."

Howard looked at Jeanine who smiled. "I'd be delighted to take her," Howard said, laughing.

"Mark. There are two Guineans who want to go. So, if you'll take them."

"Okay." Mark said, abruptly.

"That's arranged then. I suggest you start early, say two o'clock because you may have to take the longer route. The old bridge may not be passable today due to the amount of water in the river. Take a swimming suit. I'm told they have a small pool near the new club. If anyone does tricks, can tell jokes, or can sing songs or anything, they need you tonight at the club opening."

"When will the new bridge be finished, Bob?"

"It will very likely take at least another month, if the weather doesn't deteriorate too much," Bob replied.

"We'll start at two o' clock, Jeanine," Howard said, "I'll pick you up at your house."

"Okay. About the party tonight I can sing French songs, especially if someone can play a guitar."

"Okay. I'll see you at two."

CHAPTER 5

HOWARD WENT BACK to his house to pick up his bathing trunks and walked back to the annex. He waited till two o' clock and then drove his Landrover up to Jeanine's house. This was larger than the expatriates because it had two added wings made of concrete blocks and a large thatched roof in the middle. Abdul used it when he gave parties for his friends.

Jeanine was ready for the journey. She'd changed her clothes and now had on a pair of tight blue pants and white shirt. When she got in the Landrover, Howard caught the faint scent of perfume.

It was about a mile down to the River Kulu. As expected, the route to the old bridge was under water. So, they went along an old track by the side of the river. It sloped upward for three miles. The river crossing was difficult, as the water was a foot deep and the bottom was very stony. When they reached the other side, they had to go along the other bank until they reached the road near the old bridge.

"That was quite exciting," Howard said.

"That's because you've only been here a couple of weeks. It can get very annoying when it happens daily."

"How long have you lived here?" Howard asked.

"On the mine? About two years. We were the first Guineans here when the company started prospecting for diamonds. But I was actually born in Algeria in the colonial days. Afterward, my family moved to Marseilles and then to Paris. My father is an electrician. I met Abdul when I was on vacation in the Societ Union. He was doing a course with the Russian Army. Now he's in charge of the Guinean Security Department here. He's older thant me." "I was in the police force in England. A friend of mine, David Rhys, a fellow Welsh man started a Detective Agency and asked me to join him. So, I resigned from the police, put my savings into the firm and joined him. Unfortunately there wasn't enough business for two fulltime people, so when I was offered this job I took it. My wife is helping David run the busines now. I don't think I realized how tough it would be out here. Added to that, I only found out my wife was expecting a child just before I left. That worried me because my mother died just after I was born. My grandmother a primary teacher in Fishguard brought me up."

"I thought I detected a faint Welsh accent. One of my English teachers was Welsh and spoke like you."

"Yes, I went to school in Fishguard and only left Wales to join the police. But I don't say ' isn't it' anymore."

"You have a charming accent. I like it because it reminds me of Miss Rhys, my teacher."

"I'm not too worried about my wife because she comes from a large family. There were three girls and two boys and they all live around Banbury. I was the only child in my family. My father was in the army and he died a few years ago. My mother died when I was very young. I never met any of his family and only saw him occasionally after he retired from the army. I always stayed with my grandmother. I think he paid for her to look after me."

"Abdul wants to have children, but we've had no luck. I've had tests done and there aren't any problems with me, so it must be Abdul. But he's too stubborn and pig-headed to have any tests done on him. He's quite modern in most things, but in this respect he's very old-fashioned."

"It must be difficult for you sometimes." Howard was intrigued with their conversation, but didn't know Jeanine well enough to ask further questions.

They journeyed on chatting away for about an hour when Jeanine suggested they stop for a few minutes. "I've brought a flask of tea," she said. "Would you like some?"

"What a brilliant idea."

Howard parked the Landrover under a shady tree. They pulled out the seats and sat down. They were drinking their tea and nibbling on the biscuits she had brought when a Landrover came along at speed. It was Mark Buzzard. He had two passengers. There was a young Guinean girl, who looked about 16 years old sitting in the middle seat, and a younger male in the other seat. Mark stopped when he saw the Landrover. "Having trouble?" he asked.

"No just having a bit of a rest."

"Okay." Mark left in a hurry and carried on down the road to Matakourou.

"Let's carry on, Jeanine," Howard said when they had finished eating and drinking.

"Qui, Monsieur."

As they neared the mine headquarters, the road became better. Along a level area, they saw the airport. "This is near the original prospecting camp. Would you like to see it?' Jeanine asked.

"Is there anything to see?"

"Yes. You'll see how much better off you are now."

"Okay. If it's not too far."

"No. There's a road into the new camp from there. The turnoff is just there."

Howard took the smaller road she pointed out and they eventually arrived at a circle of thatched rondavels. Immediately, he noticed Buzzard's Landrover outside one of them. "I see Buzzard has arrived here."

"Yes, he likes to stay in this camp because it's free and easy," Jeanine said. "It's used to accomodate contractors and the like. There are always spare rooms. The larger building is a mess hall and bar There are two showers and flush toilets over there. In the beginning, we only had long drops as toilets. But we used to have good parties. Abdul and I never lived here but we used to come to some of the parties. You've seen enough. Let's go to the main camp."

The road nearer Matakourou was graded much better and they arrived around five o' clock. The road through the camp was coated with tarmac, so it was smooth near the club. They went into the club to inquire where they were to stay. The Campmaster went with them to show them the new Rest House. Actually, there were two new Rest Houses.

"The CEO Alec MacIntyre is staying in the one near the club and you're staying in this one here."

Howard was impressed with the speed with which the camp was being built. There were several half-finished houses near the Rest House, and the Rest House was finished. Howard parked the Landrover outside the large prefabricated building and the Campmaster ushered them in through the front door. He was obviously proud that it was finished and well furnished. "We have ten rooms here. They all have their own bathrooms. One of the stewards will be on duty till midnight tonight because of the party at the club. So, if you want something to eat or a drink, he'll be pleased to get it from the kitchen here. Breakfast will be here, but I've arranged lunch in the Club. Let me show you your rooms."

He showed Jeanine her room and gave her a key. "The generator will be on all night tonight."

She said, "Thank you," then turned to Howard. "I'll see you later on."

The Campmaster showed Howard to his room and left the building. Howard thought he'd start his stay with a beer. Noticing a small refrigerator in his room, he opened it and took out a beer. He decided not to worry about a glass. He opened it with a bottle opener he found in a drawer, sat down in a comfortable arm chair and drank it. The room was brand new, with bright yellow curtains over the windows and crimson rugs on the floor. Howard was irritated with his furnishings, comparing them with the spartan conditions he had to endure in the Banam valley.

Later, he showered and changed for dinner in the club. At six o' clock, he walked into the lounge where he found Jeanine, Dan Spring and Angeline Taylor drinking tea. He joined them and when they had finished, they walked over to the club building.

It was an impressive sight. The large concrete building looked mediaeval in the African moonlight. The group took a walk around the inside of the building. There was a large assembly room with a bar along one wall. Next to it was a smaller dining room which also had a small bar in the corner. Also there was a snooker room, a kitchen and lavatories with showers.

The assembly room was furnished with tables around three sides of the room, with a large empty space in the middle. The tables had snowy white tablecloths and silk flowers flown out from England. Howard walked into the small bar in the dining room where he found Sean McVeigh. He hadn't seen him since the lunch on the day he'd arrived. Sean invited him to spend the evening with he and his wife. Sean had been chosen to head the Security Department because of his longevity on diamond mines. However, he reminded Howard of some of the wealthy farmers he had seen in Pembrokeshire. Though he was dressed in a dinner jacket with a black tie, he looked as though he would have been more comfortable in a hacking jacket and corduroy trousers.

"We security people have to stick together," Sean said. "Maureen will be along later. What would you like to drink?"

Sean was sitting on a bar stool, so Howard pulled up another one and sat down. "I'll have a Stella beer, please."

"All the drinks are free tonight courtesy of the CEO. I think he's a bit relieved the camp is nearly finished and we're well ahead with the plant. I must say, I'm impressed with how quickly things have been arriving up that terrible road and the speed with which we've completed projects."

"I'm a complete stranger to this kind of operation and I'm amazed that anything gets finished in these kind of conditions."

"In the early days, when we were proving there were enough diamonds here, we lived in round mud huts with thatched roofs. We had communal showers and communal toilets and it really was primitive. We used to drink too much and we had rather strange ways of entertaining ourselves.

On Sundays we used to listen to the ship-to-shore messages from ships in the Mediterrean. It's very likely illegal. Mostly, we had to do the trip from Conakry by road because the Air Guinea plane wasn't always flying and that was tedious. Added to which, in the early days, every village used to have a security barrier where the villagers nearly held you to ransom. At least now, we have our own plane, with its hangar and runway. But let's get a table near the front so we can see the turns better."

They went into the big room that was now filling up with people. The room had a festive air with paper streamers hanging from the ceiling. There were ten Guinean stewards, all dressed in dazzling, white, starched uniforms behind the tables, waiting to serve drinks and food. Maureen was already seated at a table with a drink, so they joined her. There were about forty people in the room. Howard noticed five of the Guinean homologues and their wives and girlfriends sitting in a group. Normally, the Guineans didn't frequent the bar. Howard surmised it was because many of them were Muslims and also they didn't have spare money to spend. He knew most of them tried to spend their hard currency allowance on things like food or television sets with VCRs. He was pleased the company had made it open house tonight.

Howard glanced around the room. Jeanine Kourouma and Dan Spring were sitting at the same table with some of the younger mine personnel. Angeline Taylor was sitting with the Canadian Chief Executive Officer, Alec MacIntyre, the General Manager, Barry Foster and his wife Heather. The men were wearing dinner jackets and the women, long evening dresses. Howard wished he had known that some people on the mine wore dinner jackets at parties. He decided when he went back to England he would mention that more imformation about customs on the mine was neccessary for incoming employees.

When everyone had a drink, Alec MacIntyre stood to make a short speech and toast.

"When DIASA commenced three years ago, a lot of people in the diamond world said it would never produce a diamond. We didn't have enough money, equipment or expertise to do the job. But today, we're celebrating in a comfortable club. We have houses, roads, equipment and above all—you people to make the original concept possible. This camp shows what can be done with hard work and planning. But I won't take up more of your time, except to declare this club open. Please raise your glasses. To DIASA. May it prosper."

Most people stood and echoed, "To DIASA."

They sat down and the meal was served. The cooks had surpassed themselves and chicken and fish dishes were served. Afterward, there were various sweets, liquors and coffee.

The show started with a comedian. He was an engine fitter on the mine, but he wasn't a very good comedian. His jokes weren't clever enough for this audience and some of them were bawdy. But the audience clapped politely. The Guinean flame thrower inhaled when he should have exhaled and nearly set himself on fire. Still he gave a spectacular show. He was followed by Dan Spring who did some clever card tricks.

Jeanine Kourouma gave the best show of the night. She had changed into a can-can skirt with frilly petticoats underneath and had acquired an accordion from one of the Guineans. With her blonde hair and tanned skin, she looked as though she had just left the Riviera. She sang plaintive French songs in the style of Edith Piaff and also sang some of Jacques Brel's songs. The audience enjoyed her act so much, she could have gone on all night. To end her performance she danced a version of the can-can. She was accompanied by Dan on the piano. The duo got the longest applause of the evening.

Afterward, one of the homologue's wives played the piano, so that people could dance. Howard noticed the homologues and their wives were good dancers. Jeanine and Dan made a handsome couple and danced well together. Seeing the women dancing reminded him of Jean and he became a little homesick. "I'm going out for a breath of fresh air," he said to the McVeigh's.

"We're thinking of going," they said. "Goodnight. We'll see you tomorrow."

"Goodnight."

Howard went out onto the verandah and looked outside. It was a lovely moonlit night to admire the moon and stars. Later, he needed to go to the toilet, but finding it crowded decided to walk across to the Rest House. As he walked by an unfinished house, he heard two people arguing. The louder of the two, a male, was very angry and shouting.

"Why the hell did you think I gave you those drinks?"

Howard heard the sound of a slap and a short scream, and decided to investigate.

"No, no. Mr. Buzzard, please don't do that."

He walked off the road and went inside the house. Mark Buzzard was kneeling over what looked like a bundle of clothes lying on the floor. But the bundle was the young girl Mark had brought to Matakourou. She was sobbing quietly, tears coursing down her face. The sight of the frail young girl being pawed by the paunchy, middle-aged man annoyed Howard. Mark was holding her down with one hand, while trying to rip off her skirt with the other.

"What the hell are you doing? Didn't that business with the gypsy girl teach you anything? They nearly kicked you to death in Butchers Row."

Howard put his hand under Mark's shoulder, lifted him up, pulled him away from the girl and swung him around. Mark, unsteady on his feet, fell on the floor. The girl stopped crying, stood up and re-arranged her dress.

Mark stood shakily, and leaned against the wall "This is different. She's just a cheap whore. She's older than she looks."

"Don't let the locals hear you say that, or you could finish up in the river."

"What are you going to do about it?"

"This." Howard lunged forward and slammed Buzzard against the wall. He was surprised when Mark didn't fight back. One of the reasons he hadn't been liked was because he was a coward.

"You never would tackle anybody who could fight back," Howard said, contemptuously,. and released him.

"I won't forget this," Buzzard said and slunk away.

"You alright? Okay?" Mark asked the young girl, not knowing how much English she understood.

"Yes."

Howard picked up two soda cans from the ground and handed them to the girl. *What a world*, he thought. *Trying to buy a young girl for two sodas.*

"I'll take you and your brother back tomorrow. Don't go with Mr. Buzzard. Come to the Rest House at two o' clock. You understand two o' clock?" He held up two fingers.

"I understand. I learned to speak English at school. The sodas are for my father."

After two weeks in West Africa, Howard was amazed at how different people's ideas were. A girl cadging sodas for her father. *How unselfish* he thought. He patted the girl on the arm.

"Now. You've got somewhere to stay?"

"Yes. We're staying with my uncle. Mr. Buzzard said he would give me two sodas if I came to the club. I didn't know I was doing anything wrong. He said he didn't want anyone to see him giving me the sodas. That's why I came here."

"No. You didn't do anything wrong. I'll see you tomorrow. Goodnight."

The girl smiled and walked out of the building. Howard went outside and watched her walk up the road toward the club.

By now, Howard had an urgent need to go to the toilet, so he walked rapidly to the Rest House. He hurried into his room and used the bathroom. Afterward, he walked back to the club.

Except for Dan Spring, Jeanine Kourouma, Angeline and some of the younger expatriates, the club was almost empty now. Howard went into the Snooker Room to play, but the room was occupied. Mark Buzzard was lying down on one of the cushioned seats, with his arms around a young Guinean woman. Howard thought he recognized the woman from Banam, but couldn't remember who she was. The woman seemed to be enjoying Buzzard's attention. But when Buzzard saw Howard, he pulled the woman up and they left the room. Howard took a cue from the rack, chalked the end and potted a few balls.

After twenty minutes, Howard decided he was tired, so he put the cue back in the rack and went back to the Rest House. On the way, he passed the half-finished house. A ray of moonlight illuminated the interior and he was startled to see two figures silhouetted against one of the walls. He couldn't see who they were but the shadows on the walls were of a large fat man and a shorter slim female. They were wrapped around each other. The light changed and the shadows vanished. Howard hurried back to the Rest House and went to bed.

He awoke when he heard voices coming from another room. All he could make out was, "Don't make so much noise." He thought it was Jeanine's voice.

Then he went back to sleep.

He awoke again at seven o' clock and remembering about the above ground pool, he decided to start off with a swim. As he went through the lounge in his swimming trunks, carrying his towel, he was offered a cup of tea by the steward on duty. He accepted and quickly drank it. Then, in flip-flops, he walked over to the club. There was no one in the pool, so he climbed up the ladder and jumped in. He wasn't sure if it was deep enough to dive and didn't want to test it. He swam for ten minutes, dried himself with the towel and went back to the Rest House. He showered and changed into shorts and a shirt for the day. After a large breakfast, he went for a walk around the camp to see if there were any improvements since his last visit. He was impressed by how much had been done. The large prefabricated hospital was almost finished and houses were being built all over the camp. Some of the main offices were also finished.

As he was going by one of the houses, he saw the large figure of Mark Buzzard stting on a chair on the verandah. "Come and join us for a beer," He shouted.

Howard walked over. "I wouldn't mind a cup of coffee," he replied. "But I thought you stayed in the old camp last night?"

"The party in the bar there got too rough, so I left. Bring a cup of coffee," Buzzard shouted to the cook inside.

A small Guinean came out with a cup of coffee, and milk and sugar on a tray. "Good morning, Mr. Evans," he said.

"Good morning," Howard replied.

"Do you mind if I take Leila back with me today?" Buzzard asked.

"You mean the woman who was with you last night at the club."

"That's right. Her husband drives one of the gravel trucks at Banam."

"I've no objection. But don't you think her husband might object to you playing around with his wife."

"No. Tamba's not here at the moment. I don't think he knows or cares."

"Okay. I'll take Jeanine, the young girl and her brother back with me. Mrs. Taylor can go with Dan. Anyway, I'd better go now. Thanks for the coffee."

"Not at all. But lighten up. Don't be such a righteous prick. I don't care if you want the girl."

Howard went back to the Rest House. Dan Spring and Jeanine were eating a hearty breakfast of bacon and eggs at one of the dining room tables. Howard thought they made an attractive couple.

"Good morning," Howard said.

The couple looked rather startled, but replied, "Good morning."

"There's a religious service at the club this morning. There's also a British news video followed by a curry lunch at the club."

The couple did not reply.

After another cup of coffee and a piece of toast, Howard went over to the club. There was a small table with a few chairs at some distance away. Howard noticed a tall suntanned man talking to Alec MacIntyre.

"Oh, hallo, Howard. I'd like you to meet one of my compatriots, Neil Innes, who's conducting the service this morning. He's part of the Baptist Mission just outside Kissidougou. You should try and visit it if you can. They teach their students how to grow rice, as well as to be good ministers."

"Yes. If you visit, you'll get a good meal. Some of the wives there are very good cooks."

"Thanks for the invitation."

"The service will start in about five minutes. Just take one of the leaflets. We'll have a minumum of prayes and some hymns."

The service was not very long. Basically, it was just a blessing on the new club. The Smith piano provided the music. Afterward, Howard waited until the curry lunch was ready and helped himself to it. Like a lot of other people, he ate his meal sitting on the steps of the club. Growing bored, he said "Goodbye" to the McVeighs and others. He went back to his room at the Rest House and read a magazine until it was two o' clock and time to go back to Banam.

CHAPTER 6

*A*T TWO O' clock Howard was looking forward to going back to Banam. He picked up his bag, collected Jeanine Kourouma and her luggage from the lounge, and they were ready to leave. They walked outside and got into the Landrover.

"We'll pick up Francoise and her brother from the village."

They drove to the village to pick up the young girl and her brother.

"Francoise, sit in the middle," Jeanine said. "It will be more comfortable."

The young girl climbed over Jeanine and sat in the middle seat. Her brother climbed into the back of the covered Landrover. It was lucky for him, it was covered, because as they started down the road past the African village, it started to rain. It was not heavy at first, but it increased in volume and became a steady torrent.

The road from the camp became slippery. As they continued toward Banam, the road became treacherous and soft. They began to slip and slide from one side of the road to the other. Being very light, the young girl in the middle seat was bounced from Howard to Jeanine and back repeatedly. Howard found that having a passenger in the middle seat, with legs on either side of the gear lever, was distracting and made changing gears difficult. As conditions got progressively worse Howard became worried. The road had a high centre section with runnels filled with water either side. Howard wasn't used to driving in such conditions. In one swampy section, near a small stream, they became stuck in the mud. They had been running along at a good pace, but suddenly the wheels of the Landrover lost traction, carried on spinning uselessly and the vehicle stopped.

Howard got out of the cab and stepped into the pouring rain, to survey the situation. His shoes sank into the muddy road, and he was covered in a thick viscous muck up to his ankles.

"It's not too bad," he called out to Jeanine.

Francoise's brother got out of the back of the Landrover.

"Okay. If I drive," Jeanine said, "You two can push. Leila, if you get into the back, it will make it easier to drive."

The young girl got out in the pouring rain and climbed into the back of the vehicle. She was very wet by the time she sat down.

Even though Jeanine was used to these kinds of conditions, it wasn't easy to remove the vehicle from the mud. It took half an hour and several pushes to get it out. Howard and the youth used their arms and shoulders. The rear wheels sprayed up streams of muddy water and the front wheels skidded in every direction. When it was on higher ground Howard stopped for a breather. By this time the rain had stopped, and steam was rising from the ground. He and the boy were wet and plastered in mud. Jeanine produced a flask of coffee from her bag that the quartet drunk. The sun was shining and in the distance Howard could see a rainbow. But he felt as though he had boxed ten rounds in a ring.

"You'll get used to the road conditions after a few months," Jeanine said, laughing. "Just keep your sense of humour going. I'll put a small bushy branch in the road to warn the others."

Howard and the boy, Mohamed, went down to the stream to wash off some of the mud. Just as they had finished, Dan and Angeline, taking a different track, drove past without stopping. They all got back in the Landrover and continued on the road to Banam.

"I'd better drive," Howard said. "I definitely need the practice."

When they arrived at the River Kulu, they got a shock. Where the river had once been, a lake four hundred feet wide was there now. Dan's Landrover was parked under a tree at the edge of the road. Howard spotted Bob Taylor and Abdul Kourouma sitting calmly under a tree, drinking coffee. "We've been waiting for you. We've brought the rubber boat."

"I didn't think there'd be this much water," Howard said.

"It really pours at this time of year," Bob said. "Leave your Landrover on this side and we'll collect it tomorrow when the water's gone down. We have a Landrover on the other side. I suppose you haven't seen Mark Buzzard?"

"No. But if you two want to go home, I don't mind staying for Mark Buzzard and his group," Howard said.

"If that's Okay with you," Bob said.

"Thank's very much," Abdul said, walking up the bank to see his wife.

"How are you, Jeanine. Did you enjoy yourself?"

"Yes. It's a pity you didn't come."

"I had some business to attend to."

Howard parked the Landrover on top of the slope and the group walked down to where the boat was.

"Abdul, you, Jeanine and Francoise come with me and I'll bring the Landrover back," Bob Taylor said.

"No. There's no need. Remember, I have my motorcycle. If you bring the Landrover back you'd have to walk home. I'll come back."

The quartet set out. It seemed ages before Abdul came back with the boat. Howard found it difficult talking to the boy because he did not know anything about his background. He was pleased when he heard the boat coming back.

On the next trip, Howard, Abdul and the boy paddled across. They tied the boat to a tree and Abdul took Howard to the steel locker where the boat was kept.

"You'll need this key to lock the padlock," he said, handing Howard a key. Abdul and the boy then departed on the motorcycle and Howard returned to the boat. He took his time paddling back across the water, thinking how most people would have been pleased to have the kind of weekend he'd had. By this time his dirty clothes were dry and he felt more at ease in his surroundings.

It was very quiet in the patch of woodland near the river. It was dark now and moonlight filtered through the trees and cast intriguing shadows on the ground. As he waited for Mark Buzzard, Howard thought about his first two weeks in Guinea. He was still upset that the people in Banbury had not told him what conditions were like at Banam. He'd thought he would be working at Matakourou and living in a normal house. They hadn't told him that he'd be working in such an isolated place. But, he was determined to stay and finish his contract, and collect the extra promised bonus. He would not leave before the end of his six month contract.

He thought about his wife, Jean, and what the expected child would mean to them. He knew when he went home he would find it difficult to return here. He made a resolution to write her a letter tomorrow.

To pass the time, he did some of his Tai Chi exercises. When he finished, he felt more relaxed and went to sit on his log.

At 9.30, he saw headlights and heard the sound of a Landrover coming toward him. He walked up the slope and the Landrover stopped at the top of the bank. Howard went to the driver's side. Buzzard looked out bleary-eyed and asked, "How do we get across this bloody lake?" His slurred words and slale stinking breath warned Howard that he'd been drinking heavily.

"We've brought the rubber boat and have another Landrover on the other side." Howard was deliberately conciliatory and friendly. "Just turn out the lights and leave the Landrover where it is. We'll pick it up tomorrow."

"What a bloody awful trip. I nearly skid off the road a couple of times." Turning to Leila, the truck driver's wife, he said, "Come on, you stupid bitch. Let's go home."

"Well, she needs to get home before her husband arrives. You're a bloody idiot for doing something like this," Howard said. "Added to which you shouldn't have driven from Matakourou."

"Forget the sermon. Let's go home."

Buzzard staggered out of the cab and Leila climbed down from the other side. She didn't say anything, but just picked up Buzzard's hand baggage from the front of the Landrover and put it on her head. Howard made sure all the doors and windows were closed, took out the keys and put them in his pocket. They went down to the moored rubber boat. Howard positioned them in the boat, untied it from the tree and paddled them across to the other side. "Just wait while I deflate the boat," he said, pleased his day was nearly over.

Buzzard lurched out of the boat, obviously finding it difficult to stand. But Leila quickly stepped on the side of the river bank and put an arm arround Buzzard to hold him up.

"I'm not bloody waiting. I'm tired and want to go to bed. We'll walk along the path. It's much shorter. Come on, Leila," Buzzard said, slurring his speech.

Howard was too tired to argue. "Oh, suit yourself. You're an awkward sod. Goodnight. See you tomorrow."

Buzzard staggered off with his companion. Howard pulled the boat onto the bank, let the air out and folded it up. He then carried it to the steel container, put it inside and snapped the padlock shut. It had taken him fifteen minutes.

The Landrover was on the bank. He started off and drove back to his steel cabin. On the way, he thought he saw a figure moving through the trees, but quickly realized he was being influenced by the scary atmosphere of this small patch of forest. He was pleased to be home. This suprised him after his misgivings earlier. It was very hot inside, so he opened all the windows and the door. He then removed all his muddy clothes, had a quick shower and tied a towel around his waist. He found a piece of cheese in the refrigerator and cut off a portion. He cut off a piece of bread from a French baguette, married them together and ate them. He thought of how tasty the bread was in this ex-French colony. He opened a beer and drank it from the bottle. Then he removed his towel and climbed into bed.

CHAPTER 7

B Y MIDNIGHT, HE was fast asleep and dreaming. His dreams were pleasant, but muddled. He started dreaming about his childhood in Wales. He was cycling along a road under a steep hill by the side of a small river. His dream changed abruptly and he was lying in bed with his wife Jean. There was a small blonde child in a cot near the bed. The dream was so vivid he could almost smell Jean and the child.

Suddenly, he awoke and his dreams vanished. *What the hell*, he thought, aware that he was naked and the door was open. There was someone banging on the side of his cabin. He jumped out of bed, felt for his bathrobe hanging on a hook near the door and put it on.

"Wait a minute. I'm coming," he shouted. He picked up a flashlight from the table and went to the door. "Who's there?" he asked.

"Leila. Mr. Buzzard's friend."

"What's wrong?" he said, peering through the open door, and very aware of his tumescent state under his thin bathrobe.

"Mr. Evans, Mr. Evans, come quickly, please. Mr. Buzzard hasn't arrived back at his house. I've just come from there and it's still locked," she said in a rapid, breathless, high-pitched voice.

Leila was standing outside and blinked when he shone the flashlight in her face. She was sobbing and trying to push past Howard into the container. Looking at this thin, distressed girl, Howard felt sorry for her. He knew he had to find out what the problem was.

"How do you mean he isn't in his house?"

"Well, we had a fight when we left you and he hit me. So, I left him and went home. But he was drunk. Later on, I went to see how he was. He's not there. I asked around the village and no one's seen him."

"Okay. Stay there and I'll get dressed."

He wondered how a man like Buzzard could generate such concern. Howard was puzzled by the relationship between Buzzard and Leila. He surmised Buzzard and Tamba were friends, and Tamba had asked Buzzard to take Leila to Banam. *There must be some good in the man,* he thought. But he knew he was wrong. Buzzard was beyond redemption. He was an evil man.

He dressed quickly and went outside. "Let's go down the track to see if he got lost, or fell down."

He didn't take the Landrover because he didn't want to wake anyone.

The moonlight was strong enough to see by, so walking was not a problem. He had to watch his step because there were a lot of holes of differing depths scattered throughout the area. After the heavy rain the path was very soft and Howard's feet sunk into the red, sticky clay. The path was pock-marked with the footprints of previous walkers and the mud oozed over the top of his shoes. He wished he had put on his boots. There had been a short shower since he went to bed. Water dripped off the branches and leaves of the trees, soaking him. They walked back to the river but could find no sign of Buzzard.

"This forest is haunted," Leila said. "In the old days, people were frightened of passing through it at night. There's a large tree over there, with the two trunks. It's known as the devil's tree. A blood-colored sap oozes out of it when it is cut, or a branch breaks off. Some of the old people believe you can use the sap to put a curse on your enemy. A few weeks ago, it fell down. We had a terrible storm. It rained a lot and the wind was very strong. Mr. Buzzard was walking along here after it stopped raining and it nearly hit him when it fell. It left a large hole and the roots are showing."

"You speak very good English, Leila!"

"I went to school in Freetown, when I was young."

"Is it possible Mr. Buzzard went somewhere else?" he asked, hoping she would agree. But she didn't. "No. He was very drunk, bad tempered and only wanted to go to bed."

They retraced their steps toward the village, but walked more slowly and examined the vegetation along both sides of the track. Half way along, near the devil's tree just off the track on the road side, they found Buzzard's body. He was lying half in and out of a hole. He was head first into the hole, with his feet sticking out.

"Is he dead?" Leila screamed She threw herself on the ground and clutched at the protruding feet, making a trilling noise and beating herself with her fists.

"Get up, Leila, and stop that noise."

Leila hastily scrambled to her feet and Howard shone his flashlight into the hole.

Buzzard's grey hair was illuminated by the light. He was five feet away from the track, lying face down in a small rocky hole that was partially filled with water. The top of the hole was obscured by grass and weeds growing in the soil around it. It looked as though it was a hole dug by diggers looking for diamonds a long time ago. Buzzard's head was above the water. It was lying on loose rocks covering the bottom of the pit. Howard could see he was dead by his stillness and rigidity. He climbed down the boulders into the hole and felt the body for a pulse. There wasn't any sign of one and the body was cool.

When he climbed out, he shone his flashlight around the edges of the pit. All he could see were muddy footprints and motorcycle tracks.

"He's dead. He must have fallen down the hole. We'll go back and you can go home. I'll go tell Mr. Taylor." He put his hand on Leila's arm and led her back up the track. When she was moving, he released her arm and they walked to the village. "You alright now?" He asked Leila.

"Yes. I'll go home now."

"Okay. I'll see you in the morning. Goodnight, Leila."

"Goodnight, Mr. Evans. You're a good man." She walked into the village.

Howard carried on up the road to the manager's house. He knocked, loudly, on the front door. It was very dark inside the house. "Who's there?" He heard Bob Taylor's voice coming from one of the bedrooms at the side of the building. A window opened wider.

"Howard Evans, here. I'm afraid I've got bad news. Mark Buzzard has had an accident and is dead."

"Good God. Okay. I'm coming."

Howard heard Bob say, "No, no. Don't you get up I'll handle it."

There was the glow of a battery lamp inside. Eventually the front door was opened and Bob Taylor came down the steps dressed in a shirt and slacks. He was carrying a Polaroid camera. "We may as well get some photographs tonight before things are messed up."

They climbed into Bob's Landrover and drove down the road. "It should be about here," Howard said. They stopped the Landrover on the road and walked through the shrubby bush to the track where the pit was.

Once again, Howard shone his flashlight on the body.

"He's definitely dead?" Bob asked.

"Definitely."

Bob handed Howard his Polaroid camera. "You're the ex-policeman. Take some pictures and we'll leave him here till tomorrow. I don't think we want to move him until we've informed the Guinean authorities."

"I'll send some security men to watch the body and the area and I'll send a tarpaulin in case it rains," Howard said.

"Okay. We can't do anymore till tomorrow. You arrange your security men and I'll radio Matakourou tonight."

Howard took and developed the ten Polaroid photographs left in the camera. He used flash lighting and got photographs of the body and immediate area around the pit. They walked back to the Landrover. Bob drove up the road to the Security Post near the village. He stopped at the Sergeant's newly completed house. It was an impressive mud and concrete building with a aluminium roof. "Sekou, Sekou," Howard shouted, as he banged on the door.

After long time, the door was opened. "Oh, it's you, Mr. Evans. What's happened?"

"There's been an accident along the track to the river. Mr. Buzzard is dead. Get two other security men and come with me. I want you to guard the body till tomorrow morning Also, send someone to look after his house."

"Okay. Mr Evans."

"I'll walk back to the camp," Bob said. "Just arrange the guards and I'll see you in the morning. Come to the office at seven o' clock and I'll find out what we must do."

Bob walked back up the road to his office to use his radio.

Howard drove to his office, opened up the store and found a tarpaulin. He put this in the back of the Landrover. Howard took his men back to the accident site. There was a lone figure sitting on a rock by the side of the pit. It was Leila. "I couldn't leave him by himself. So, I came back."

The men covered the pit with the canvas cover.

"Make sure no one comes along to rob the body and it's safe from animals."

"You can trust us."

"Okay. Goodnight. You can come with me now, Leila."

They walked back to the Landrover when he heard the sound of a motorcycle coming down the track from the village. H returned to the pit. The Suzuki motorcyle rider stopped when he saw the men. He got off the motorcycle, put it on its stand and came toward them. "What's happened? Why are you here?"

"Mr. Buzzard's had an accident. He's dead," the sergeant said.

"Why are you here?" Howard asked Tamba, the assistant witchdoctor and truck driver.

"I've been away for the weekend. When I went home Leila wasn't there. So I looked around the village. When I couldn't find her, I came along the path because someone said she'd gone to Matakourou."

"Where did you spend the weekend, Tamba?" Howard asked.

"I went to stay with some friends down south. They owed me some money. I just got back tonight."

Howard decided he would question him in the morning.

"I'll come and see you at work tomorrow. Go home now. I'll drop off Leila."

He drove Leila to the village and dropped her off at her home. He then drove back to his house. He decided not to wake Abdul and Jeanine, but to tell them of the death the next morning.

He was very tired and slept soundly for the rest of the short night.

CHAPTER 8

THE NEXT MORNING he showered, dressed. ate a quick breakfast and walked down to his office just before seven a.m.

"Any messages?" he asked the radio operator.

"Just one a few minutes ago. The helicopter is coming for Mr. Buzzard's cases and the body. The company is sending a new Plant Security Officer from Matakourou and the Guinean authorities are sending a police officer to replace Mr. Abdul who's to work with you. I've written the messages down." The operator handed Howard a piece of paper which he read.

"Good man."

Adbul arrived and they walked into Howard's office. He was upset.

"Howard, Why wasn't I told of Buzzard's death. last night?"

"Well it was very late and I knew we couldn't do anything at that time of night. Let's go and see Bob Taylor."

Howard decided to talk to Bob Taylor before the helicopter arrived. He was unsure what the company wanted him to do concerning Mark Buzzard's death and what the Guinean authorities would do about it. He thought the death must have been an accident because of the circumstances. It couldn't have been anything else. He walked to Bob Taylor's office and waited for him to arrive. Bob arrived just before seven a.m, unlocked the door to his office and went inside. Howard heard him switch on the radio.

"Morning, Howard. Oh, hello, Abdul, Come inside,." Bob said.

"What's Matakourou want us to do about Mark Buzzard?" Howard asked.

"That's why I'm here. I've received a radio message. They're sending a helicoptor for the body. We're lucky they hired one for Alec MacIntyre's visit. He's been using it to view the lease area and possible mining areas. Also, he wanted to see if he they would be useful detering illegal diggings in the bush."

"Okay. We'll just sit and wait for the helicoptor."

"Who knows about the death so far?" Howard asked.

"Officially?. Here, us and the radio operator. Also, Matakourou know. Unofficially, everybody knows. I couldn't contact the doctor last night because he was away from the mine. The Guinean doctor was at Matakourou visiting friends and we couldn't find him. I'll get a notice printed, telling people what has happened—everybody at the various sites."

"Matakourou will have told Conakry. So, the people in Banbury must know. But we will need a death certificate from the doctor to accompany the body to England," Howard said.

They didn't have long to wait. The helicopter arrived with a cacophony of noise and clouds of leaves and debris. A crowd of children hurried from the village to see the show. The helicopter landed on the large open space in front of the future Security compound.

"We'd better go to meet it," Bob said, resignedly. "It's going to be one of those days."

He and Howard hurried over to the helicopter. As they arrived, the rotors were switched off and Alec MacIntyre descended from the craft, followed by Sean McVeigh. The pilot came round from the other side.

"Hallo, Bob. I was horrified to hear the news about Mark Buzzard," Alec said. "Do we know what happened yet?"

"It looks like he wandered off the track, tripped over a rock or something and fell into an old pit," Howard said. "He smelled of drink when he arrived at the river. I tried to get him to wait for me, but he was very bad-tempered and wanted to get to bed. I thought the woman with him would see he got home. It's not a long walk."

"Well, I'd like you to take statements from anyone who was around at the time. We must give Banbury the full picture. There'll be an inquest in England and I want to be prepared for any questions. I'm not too sure what the Guinean authorities will do. Lieutenant Momoh will assist Adbul with his security duties when he arrives. I'd like Abdul to work with you. Remember to give him all the information you get. A new man, Henry Hardcastle, is the replacement for Mark Buzzard. He'll be arriving from Matakourou later on. He's a very solid individual."

"I'll do what I can," Howard said. "He can stay in the Rest House until we clean up Mark's house."

Jeanine arrived. She chatted to the pilot and Sean MacVeigh, and then she and Abdul returned to their house with them.

"Today," Alec said, "I'd like to take Mark's body back to Matakourou because we have to send the helicopter back to Freetown. The Cessna can take the coffin down to Conakry tomorrow for London. Howard, how's your French?'

"I speak it quite well."

"Good. Because I'd like you to go down to Conakry to deal with any formalities. The Conakry manager will help. I'm going to London on the same plane, so there shouldn't be any problems. The British Embassy is sending us the right type of metal coffin for the journey to London. The coffin will arrive today and you can fill it tomorrow morning. If you get your things you can fly back with us."

"Okay. I'll meet you back here or at the accident site."

"Bob, you can come with us to the accident site. We've brought a stretcher to transport the body on the skid."

Howard walked back to his house, packed a change of clothes, pajamas and a shaving kit in a leather bag, and returned to the Security compound. The helicopter had left. But it returned about half an hour later with Mark Buzzard's body strapped underneath.

Bob Taylor got out and Howard got into the helicopter.

"Well, Goodbye, Bob. I'll see you again sometime," MaeIntyre said. "I appreciate how difficult your job is sometimes. Goodbye, Sean. I'm sorry there's no more room in the helicopter." "It's Okay. Somebody's got to take the Landrover back when the two Security men arrive," Sean said. "Goodbye, Sir. Have a good trip."

Watched by a crowd of cheering and waving children the helicopter took off, and swung round in the direction of Matakourou. The helicopter arrived there before nine am.

Again, there was a crowd to meet them at the Security Headquarters.

"We have a large freezer where we can keep the body till tomorrow morning," Alec MacIntyre said. "The metal coffin has arrived and we'll load it on a lorry tomorrow morning for the airport. I didn't like Mark Buzzard too much, but I'm sorry to see him finish up like this."

"Yes. It must be horrible to die alone in such circumstances. Did he have any children?"

"No. He was divorced ten years ago and there were no children. Apparantly, he did help to support his father. He has an old person's flat in Banbury. The company will pay him the insurance money. You are staying the night at the Rest House. It will make it easier to load up tomorrow. We're going together, anyway. The freezer is in the store over there. We'll keep the generator running. Let's get the body in the freezer."

There were two security men standing by the helicopter.

"Tamba, Saa. Let's carry the body into the store." Howard said.

The men looked rather apprehensive, but gingerly picked up the stretcher which had been untied by the pilot and his assistant. They carried it into the store.

"Put it one this table, so I can examine it," the Guinean doctor who was waiting in the store wearing rubber gloves said.

He cursorily examined the clothed body, looking for obvious signs of the cause of death. "The blow to the head obviously killed him,." he said.

"Any idea how it was caused?" Howard asked.

"No. We'll need a pathological examination to do that. But I will issue a death certificate, so the body can be sent to England. You can put it in the freezer now."

"Thank you, doctor," Alec MacIntyre said, rather formally.

Howard and Alec followed.

"Lift the stretcher up and we'll lower the body inside."

It was done very quickly and the body was surrounded by ice blocks.

"That should be alright until tomorrow. The metal coffin is over there and we have a lightweight wooden coffin inside." Alec pointed to a large wooden crate.

"Tamba, Saa make sure you're here early tomorrow morning. We have to load the body onto the lorry. We have a fork lift loader here and at the airport."

Alec and Howard left in a chauffered Mercedes-Benz for the Rest House.

"I'm glad we've got the body away from Banam. That place is too small and isolated to cope too well with a tragedy like this," Alec said.

"Yes. I think six months at a place like that is enough," Howard said. "There's not enough entertainment. The houses need to be bigger and we need more couples to stabilize the place. I'd like to bring Jean out here for a visit, but Banam is too primitive. Think what would have happened if Mark Buzzard had only been seriously injured? That trip from Banam would be a nightmare. I understand it took a long time to find the doctor last night."

Alec did not reply.

The Mercedes stopped at the Rest House where Howard had previously stayed. A uniformed servant came down the steps to see if there was anything that needed to be carried inside.

"Good afternoon, Mr Evans. Can I take your bag inside?"

"Yes, Amadou. Mr. Evans will be staying the night," Alec said. "Show him to his room."

The steward took Howard's bag from him and carried it into the house. They walked through the verandah into the lounge, along a passageway. The man showed him to the same room he'd had previously.

"Thank you," Howard said.

"If you need anything, just call me."

"You should be comfortable here. It has its own bathroom." Alec said when he went outside again. "I'll see you tomorrow morning. I'm busy for the rest of the day."

"Thanks. I'm sorry to be such a nuisance."

"I'm meeting Maureen, Sean's wife, at the club now. We're meeting with some of the wives to discuss future events there. We want to establish a sense of community similiar to what we had in Sierra Leone."

"Surely the situation is a little different here," Howard said. "That was a well established ex-colonial company going back a long way. They did things differently. Here, we have a smaller expatriate group and could have a mixed club for them and the Guineans."

"Your trouble is, Howard, you never worked in places like Kenya or Sierra Leone in the old days. Anyway, I must go. You can go for a swim at the club, or watch VCRs on the television in the lounge. If you want anything, just call Amadou."

Howard spent the morning swimming in the small pool at the club. At lunchtime, he went back to the Rest House for lunch. In the afternoon, he watched VCRs on the television set in the lounge.

Maureen McVeigh walked in about four o' clock.

"How are you, Howard? Would you like to come to our house for some tea? I'm not sure when Sean will be in. Alec MacIntyre has been touring the mine with him. He's been asking a lot of questions."

"I wouldn't mind a cup of tea," Howard said.

They walked down the road to the McVeigh's house.

Maureen ushered Howard into an armchair on the verandah.

She went to the kitchen and came back a few minutes later with a tray with tea things on it and a plate of homemade scones.

"Do you like strawberry jam? It's homemade."

"Yes, please."

While they were eating they discussed their experiences on the mine.

"You must find living out at Banam very strange after Banbury?"

"Yes. It is very frustrating. But, it wouldn't be difficult to make it better. Larger living quarters would help. Also, because of our small numbers, social events with the Guineans would help. Look how we enjoyed Jeanine's performance the other night."

"I don't think the company would agree. I think they're afraid there might be conspiracies to steal diamonds if the two groups got too friendly. Oh! Before I forget, I'm giving a dinner tonight. The Fosters are coming and Jim and Cathie Green are representing the younger crowd. You are invited and can entertain Alec with stories about the Banbury police. He was in the Canadian Mounties when he was young."

At dinner, Alec talked to Howard about the Royal Canadian Mounted Police.

"As an ex-British policeman, you could join," Alec said. "I'm sure you'd do well. It's worth thinking about for the future. Give me a call, in Winnipeg, if you ever consider it."

He wrote a number on one of his business cards and gave it to Howard.

"That's my home number, so don't give it to anyone else. I think you would do well in Canada. There are a lot of opportunities there. This mine is our first venture outside North America. Our main mining activities are over there. We were asked to start this mine here and got a good deal tax-wise. But, it is an unsual operation for us. It should be very profitable to my company. If the mine is successful and we discover a lot of diamonds, we might sell out to a bigger corporation."

As though realizing he had said too much, Alec stopped talking to Howard and started talking to Jim Green's good-looking blonde wife, Cathie, on his other side.

"Come here for breakfast tomorrow morning. We'll have breakfast at six am,. so the plane can leave before 7:30. We have to load up the coffin, so we can't be late. Good Night," Sean said.

After a very good dinner the guest left and Howard went to the Rest House and bed.

CHAPTER 9

*H*OWARD WAS READY by 6.00 am. and walked over to the MacVeigh's house. Sean was already eating breakfast when he arrived.

"You're up early," Howard said.

"Well, we have a lot to do if the plane is to take off at 7.30."

When they arrived at Security Compound, Tamba and Saa were already there.

Sean parked the Landrover, and he and Howard went inside to the storeroom. On the way, Howard put his leather bag into the cab of the lorry.

"This is the one for the airport?" he asked Sean.

"Yes. but let's load Buzard into the metal coffin for the plane flight. First, we'll get him into the wooden coffin, screw it down and then lock him in the metal coffin. There's a wooden crate at the airport. That way, no one on the International flight need know there's a coffin on board."

Howard was surprised how quickly they emptied Buzzard out of the freezer, into the wooden coffin and then into the metal coffin. He realized people were not callous. Rather, they were embarrassed to have to treat a dead person in such a brusque manner. A forklift truck took the assembly to the lorry. Howard thought how ignominious it was for the dead man.

Howard and Sean followed the lorry to the small airport, with its red laterite runway and large hangar. The hangar was very necessary in the rainy season to stop passengers from being soaked. They drove inside the hangar where the plane was parked. A forklift truck loaded the coffin into the wooden crate and took it to the plane. Sean had ten men ready to help load the crate into the small plane. This was difficult due to the small door but it was eventually done. Most of the seats had been removed to accommodate the crate. Howard and Alec MacIntyre had two seats on either side of the plane in the rear. The pilot handed Howard a flask of coffee and a container of milk.

"In case you get thirsty. Howard, I hope you've brought an overnight bag because we may have to wait for an urgent spare part at the airport. Sometimes, they take days to release things. But this one is very urgent because it's needed at Banam."

"Yes, I've brought a bag," Howard said.

"Good. We have rooms booked for tonight at the Independence, "the pilot said.

The Guinean co-pilot said, "We'd better get going."

"Okay, Jean."

The plane was pushed out of the hangar and took off at precisly 7.30 am. They set a course for Conakry.

When they had levelled off, Howard glanced through the window. He was an little uneasy because of the coffin in front of him. He was intrigued by an area near a large river below them. The area was pock-marked with excavations of varying sizes, from small to huge. The pilot swooped down, so they could see better. The area was like a beehive, or ant's nest with workers digging and carrying away baskets of earth.

"They're digging for diamonds, but this isn't in the DIASA lease area," Alec said. "One of the problems in Guinea is that some of the diamonds are in pockets which are very rich, but difficult to discover and extract with machinery."

"Why don't the Guinean authorities stop it?"

"They don't need to. It could be a licensed area. The government will collect a tax on the diamonds recovered."

Howard tried to imagine what it must be like living in a community of mixed nationalities, all engaged in trying to strike it rich. *It must be difficult just to survive.*

"We thought of mining here, but thought it must have been worked out. We may have been wrong. Years ago, the old Selection Trust Company had plants in Guinea. There was one near here. Our reasoning was that the best areas must have been worked out."

"What happened during the war when the Vichy government was allied to the Germans?"

"There's an interesting story about that period. There were two Irish brothers working for the company at that time. I can't remember their names. It was something like Moody or Murphy. One of them, disguised as an African, took the diamonds from his plant in Guinea all the way to Yengema in Sierra Leone. I heard the story some years ago when I was staying at a London hotel. One of the brothers was working as a consultant for Selection Trust. There's also another story about another manager of a small, high quality diamond plant who disappeared. No one knows quite what happened to him because he didn't reach Sierra Leone and was never heard of again."

"What happened to his diamonds?" Howard asked.

"They never turned up—unless they were cut and sold outside the usual markets—which seems unlikely."

"Is it possible the manager took them and just went to live somewhere else, like South Africa."

"No. It was wartime, so he'd have had trouble travelling there without proper documents, or papers."

"I thought the experts could tell which countries produced a particular diamond by its characteristics?"

"I believe so."

Howard could tell Alec didn't want to carry on the conversation so kept quiet.

He glanced out of the window at the endless rocky outcrops and green grass, with the occasional village.

Nearer to Conakry, the country became wetter and they saw more rice fields. In a large pond, they saw a group of women fishing. They were bare from the waist upwards and their skirts were tucked in and tied around their waists. They were using weighted nets which they threw expertly onto the surface of the water. Howard didn't see them retrieve any fish, but he did see silver streaks which indicated fish, in the water. The women waved at the plane.

They landed at Conakry International Airport after a two hour flight. The airport looked huge from the small plane. They taxied to the cargo area. Pierre Beauregard, the Canadian Conakry manager, was waiting for them. He was six feet tall, with grey hair and sun-tanned skin.

"Mr. MacIntyre, we have everything arranged to send the body to England. I'll give you the papers when you're ready to leave. You won't have to worry about anything. I've arranged for it to be collected from Heathrow for transport to Oxford. They'll do the autopsy there and arrange for the Coroner's inquest."

"Thanks, Pierre. I'm glad you're working here. My regards to Marie." Alec then glanced at Howard. "Goodbye, Howard. I'll do something about the lack of a doctor at Banam. Perhaps a well expeienced nurse would be the answer? Think what I said about Canada. I'm afraid I have to meet someone here."

"I will think about what you said."

Alec walked away.

"I'm Pierre Beauregard, the Conakry Manager," Pierre introduced himself. "And you're Howard Evans. I don't think I met you when you arrived a couple of weeks ago."

"No, you were at a meeting or something."

"Very likely. We have meetings all the time. You're having lunch with me and my wife, Marie. You're in luck. We know of a very good restaurant owned by a French lady that serves up some of the best food in West Africa. She's a partly Guinean and married to a Frenchman. I don't know what happened to him. Possibly better not to ask. Bring your bag and I'll see about the spare parts for the mine."

Pierre went through a glass door into the airport. The door was narrow, with a magnetic security arch. Howard was later on told that the arch was not connected to the electrical supply. Inside it was very dark in the old hangar-style building. Howard remembered how strange he;d felt when he arrived from England, but the friendleness and helpfulness of the Guineans had allayed his anxities. Howard was amazed by the number of people inside. He could not imagine that they were all travellers, or friends of travellers, but realized they had to be.

Just beyond the arch was a series of offices; health, immigration, and the like. Howard remembered how distrustful he had been when he arrived from England and a DIASA employee had taken his passport and other documents. He expected someone to steal them. For some strange reason, though, the system worked. His documents were all stamped and his luggage retrieved and stowed in the company bus, as if by magic, to be transported to the hotel.

Pierre led the way up a flight of steps.

"I'll leave you in the lounge, while I see about the body and Mr. MacIntyre's departure. You can sit in a chair over there. Would you like some coffee?"

"Yes, please."

Pierre beckoned one of the stewards overand spoke to him in rapid French which Howard found difficult to follow. "I'll see you later. They'll look after you." He then went down the stairs into the luggage area.

Howard was ushered into a large leather chair by the steward, who then left and came back with a tray with a coffee cup, saucer, spoon and milk on it.

Pierre returned at ten o' clock.

"You'll have to stay the night. I can't get the plant spares until tomorrow. Have a beer, if you feel like it."

"I think I will. A Stella, please."

The steward brought the beer and Pierre disappeared again.

At 11 o' clock, the UTA plane took off. Shortly afterward, Pierre came back. He picked up Howard's bag. "Come on, let's go to my house."

They walked down the stairs to the exit and went outside to Pierre's Peugot station wagon.

"Did Alec MacIntyre get off Okay?"

"Yes. He's gone and Buzzard, also."

It was about half an hour to Pierre's house, which overlooked a small beach. On the way, Pierre told Howard how he and Marie came to be in Conakry. "I was with the Free French forces during the war and met Alec in England. He was with the Canadian forces. After the war, he persuaded me to go to Canada. When he started this company, he offered me the job of Conakry Manager because I speak French. Marie is Canadian."

"I was with the Thames Valley Police before I came here," Howard said. "I find it very different to what I'm used to."

"You'll get used to it after a bit and the pay's good."

The road from the airport was tarred and consisted of two lanes in either direction. There was an operational railway on one side of the road. Howard was surprised by the heavy traffic, of cars, buses and lorries.

On the way Pierre asked about Buzzard's accident. "How did it happen?"

"No one's quite sure yet what happened. We're hoping to learn more when they do the autopsy in Oxford. Abdul, my Guinean Security homologue, is questioning some of the Guinean staff today and I'll queston the expatriates when I get back. Basically, he fell into an old pit dug by somebody years ago. He had been drinking all day and was very drunk."

The Peugot pulled up in a small driveway.

"We'll leave your bag inside and drive to the Independence hotel after lunch."

"Would it be possible to telephone my wife in England?" Howard asked.

"It is theoretically possible, but it would take all day. The best thing is to write her a letter and I'll give it to someone going to England or Europe tomorrow morning. Placing an overseas call using the present system is very slow. Let's go inside."

They walked around the side of the small single storey house, past neat flower beds, up concrete steps onto a louvred windowed verandah. Mrs. Beauregard was sitting in a comfortable—looking armchair reading a Paris Match magazine. She put it down and motioned Howard to sit in another armchair.

"Like a beer, Howard?" Pierre asked.

Howard wasn't used to drinking before lunch, so he declined. "No. I think a soft drink would be better."

Pierre fetched him a lemonade drink and another for himself.

They sat down and chatted until twelve o' clock.

"Well, let's go and eat," Marie said, standing up. "I'll take some wine though because Fifi charges the earth for her cheap wines."

She went into the kitchen and returned carrying a cloth bag. The two men followed her outside to the Peugot. Pierre drove and this time they finished up on a tree-lined, side street in the suburbs of Conakry. The small restaurant was on a corner, the wide pavement outside filled with tables and shaded by the trees. They parked the car by the side of a table, got out and sat. It was a pleasant sunny day, with a soft breeze and feathery clouds providing coolness and shade.

A comely, brown-skinned, middle-aged woman came out of the restaurant. She embraced Marie and Pierre and shook hands with Howard.

"This is possibley the most authentic French restaurant in Conakry," Pierre said.

"He's one of the most authentic flatterers in Conakry," the woman said, smiling. "But remember, he was born in Paris."

"No. No. I really mean it. What have you got for us today?"

Well, I've got some fresh fish bought this morning—straight from the ocean. I've given them a West African flavour with a peppered sauce I've made."

"You should try this, Howard," Pierre said, almost smaking his lips. "Fifi is famous for her hot fish."

"I'd love to try it, Howard said.

"You know we'll try it," Marie said.

"Will you start with the soup, or the salad?"

"The salad for me, Howard said.

"For us, as well," Pierre said.

Marie Beauregard reached down and pulled out a bottle of red wine from her bag and put it on the table. Fifi looked at her, sighed and frowned.

"I suppose you won't want any wine?" Fifi said, without getting an answer said. "I'll go and start the meal." She walked into the restaurant.

A waiter came out with three glasses. Marie produced a corkscrew, pulled the cork from the bottle of wine and poured it into the glasses.

"A votre sante," Pierre proposed, lifting his glass. The others echoed the toast and they all drank.

Howard thought how pleasant it was sitting outside and drinking wine. Then remembered why he had come to Conakry and felt a little sad for Buzzard. He also wondered if he had ever come to this restaurant.

The meal was excellent and they finished with coffee and French cheeses.

Pierre didn't pay cash for the meal. Instead he signed the bill to be debitted from the DIASA account.

Howard went inside to use the toilet. Inside, the restaurant was very plain with oil cloth table coverings. The walls were painted green and white. The toilet was clean and smelled of carbolic soap. Again, it was plain, consisting only of foot rests. It did have flushing water though. There was a washbasin outside with only cool water.

"Au revoir," the trio said to Madame Fifi.

"Au Revoir," she replied. smiling. "Hope to see you again," she said to Howard.

This time, they drove to the Independence Hotel with its tennis courts and sea view. The Beauregards dropped Howard at the front door.

"We'll see you again. I'll see you tomorrow morning," Pierre said, opeing the door into the hotel. "I'll send a car at nine o' clock. Don't be late."

"Goodbye," Fifi said.

"Goodbye."

Howard walked through the glass doors up to the desk. Pierre closed the door and the Beauregards left.

"Have you a room for Evans?" Howard asked.

"Certainly, Sir. Will you please fill in this form? DIASA has booked a room."

Howard completed the form. The Guinean clerk glanced at it.

"Room 202," he said to Howard and gave him a key.

Howard took the lift up to the first floor and walked along the corridor until he found room 202. He opened the door and went inside. It was a typical modern hotel room, with attached bathroom and TV. He put his bag on the luggage stand and sat down in one of the two armchairs. The room was air-conditioned and cool compared to the heat outside. Relaxed, he thought about his changed circumstances since the previous night. Then, he was bemoaning his primitive accommodation and now he was staying in the best hotel in Conakry. He'd had a pleasant day.

Thinking about his trip made him also think about Buzzard's death. If it wasn't an accident, then who had killed him? Buzzard's casual treatment of women might suggest an irate male.

Tired and relaxed in the comfortable chair, he nodded off to sleep. He had an unusual dream. He saw a young, unshaven, tired man riding a large, old-fashioned motorcycle along a muddy road. But he was so tired, he couldn't control the bike. He skidded in the mud and the bike fell on top of him.

Howard awoke, he realized his dream was about the story Alec had told him concerning the old Guinea diamond mine.

About six pm. he showered and changed into slacks and a clean shirt. He walked along the corridor into the bar. He ordered a Konigsbourg beer and signed the chit, DIASA. He looked around the bar. Most of the patrons were white. He surmised they were either diplomats, business men, or executives of charity organizations. He started a conversation with the man next to him and discovered he worked at the British Embassy in Conakry. He introduced himself. "I'm Jim Brown and work at the British Embassy here."

"Howard Evans. I'm with DIASA the diamond company up near Kissidougou."

"Yes, I've heard about you. Your UK office is in Banbury. Though most of the capital seems to be Canadian or American."

"Yes. We're pretty international."

"Didn't one of your people die last week?"

"Yes. On Sunday. That's why I'm here. I accompanied the body to Conakry. He's on the plane to London today."

Brown looked at his watch. "Well, I have to go now. There's a party at the French Embassy. See you around."

"Goodbye."

Around seven pm, he went downstairs and walked to the outside restaurant with the view of the lighthouse.

The food was similar to what one would get in a good restaurant in Paris. Howard sat at a table, having a good view of the palm trees and the beach. He ordered a glass of wine and the peppered fish dinner. Afterward, he finished his meal with coffee and a brandy. He wrote his room number and DIASA on the bill, signed it and walked back inside.

He walked upstairs to the bar. When he got there, he decided not to go in. He returned to his room. He phoned the front desk to book an early call for seven am, and turned on the television. The picture was hazy, so he turned it off. He then decided he must write a to his wife for delivery tomorrow. Once he started writing, he carried on until he had filled four pages of the hotel's notepaper found in the desk drawer.

He told his wife about the 'accident', realizing that in a small town like Banbury the news would soon spread. He could imagine *The Banbury Guardian* writing a column about the death of a former policeman, especially as DIASA's office was on the Oxford road. If the Banbury office was quick, they would have already have told the local newpapers. Presumably, MacIntyre would have informed the Coroner's office. When Howard had finished his letter. he went to bed.

The comfortable bed and large air-conditioned room soon sent him to sleep. Just before he dozed off, he thought how different it would be if the accommodations at Banam were as comfortable.

In the morning he awoke before he got the early morning call. He showered, shaved and dressed, and then answered his early call. He went downstairs to have breakfast in the dining room. He returned and packed his bag, ready for his trip to Matakourou. He then went downstairs to the reception desk. There he signed his account and waited for his lift to the airport. The lobby had some very comfortable, leather armchairs.

At 8.30 am, a uniformed driver came into the lobby and called out, "Mr. Evans!"

"That's me," he informed him, with a smile.

The man picked up Howard's bag and he followed him out to a station wagon. The weather was good. There was a cooling breeze and it wasn't too hot.

The drive to the airport was without incident, but Howard was a little apprehensive. The driver was erratic. The roads were crowded and occasionally, to speed up, his driver would drive on the wrong side of the dual carriageway. The first time it happened, he wondered if the man was insane. The second time, he saw it coming when they came to an empty section. On the way the man pointed out the famous bridge over the road where several people were executed some years prior. Howard didn't know too much about the recent history of Guinea, so he didn't say anything. He visualized struggling bodies being thrown off the bridge. Eventually, they arrived at the airport. He saw Pierre Beauregard waiting near the entrance and gave him the letter to send to England.

"I'll see it goes. I hope I'll see you again sometime."

"Goodbye, Pierre. I enjoyed lunch yesterday. It was quite an experience."

The pilot and the co pilot came round to take his luggage and escort him to the plane. They took off at 9.30am, and flew to Matakourou. The weather was sunny with a few clouds, so it was a pleasant flight.

Sean MacVeigh was waiting in his Landrover at the airport and took him back to his house. Howard had a rather plain lunch with Sean and Maureen and then decided to return to Banam. Sean had a Landrover waiting to take him back to Banam.

First, he decided to do some shopping at the Provision store. The store consisted of a series of containers, each fitted out with steel shelves that were joined together. The store was open from nine o' clock in the morning till six o' clock in the evening. The inhabitants of Banam had a pet peeve about the store because the wives in Matakourou, who would see the arrival of the food trucks, would select the more attractive provisions before the Banam people were informed of their arrival. So many times they would finish up with strangely shaped pieces of meat which were too long for their small ovens. Things such as fruit and vegetables from Europe were not allocated to Banam.

He drove to the new Provision store, with its impressive turnstile entrance, and obtained some meat and fish to take back to Banam. He obtained cold boxes plugged into the battery to keep the food refrigerated.

Several people came up to him in the store to talk about Buzzard's death. They all talked about the accident. He could tell they were all glad it had happened at Banam. Francoise's brother, Mohamed, was waiting for him when he came out of the store.

"Will you take me back to Banam, please, Mr. Evans?"

"Yes, certainly, Mohamed. Are you ready?"

"Yes. I heard you were here and brought my things."

"Okay. Let's go."

They both got in the front of the Landrover. This time the trip to Banam was uneventful. The road was drying up and he didn't get stuck anywhere. But the river was still flooded and they needed the collapsible boat. Abdul Kourouma was waiting for them and took them across in the boat. He had brought a driver who would drive the long way back to Banam. "It should be shallow enough at the top end," he said. "Otherwise, he'll have to wait at the other crossing. He won't mind that."

After they had locked up the boat, Abdul drove to the Security Post. Howard could see he was eager to tell him the result of his investigations. Mohamed said, "Goodbye," and left. Abdul led the way into the office.

"I've got statements from Tamba and Leila and I've tranlated them into English and French. I want to be ready for the inquiry here and presumably, there'll be an inquest in England.? I want to ready for any eventuality."

"You seem to be thinking of all possible problems?"

"Well, we have to satisfy the Guinea government and DIASA. So, we'd better get all the facts we can."

"Yes, I suppose you're right. But what have you learned so far?"

"Tamba says what he said before. He was there only looking for his wife. He said he didn't see anyone on the road. Anyway, Buzzard had been dead for some hours when Tamba arrived."

"What did Leila say?. She told me Buzzard hit her and she ran back to the village,". Howard said.

"She repeated the same story. Buzzard suddenly got angry, hit her, and she ran to her house in the village. But this time she embellished the story.

She now says that she had the idea there was someone hiding in the bushes. But she's very unsure about it and may be trying to help her husband."

"I wonder why Buzzard suddenly flew into a rage. I know he was a bad-tempered sort of person, but when I saw him he seemed to be in a good mood. He was obviously very drunk."

"Yes. That's worth investigating. Why did he fly into a rage? Did he want to get rid of Leila for some reason?" Abdul asked.

"What was Tamba doing on Saturday and Sunday?"

"He says he went to collect a debt. We think he's lying. But I'm waiting for a report from the police at Beyla. They'll find out why he was there. The fact that it's connected with a murder will speed up things. The people down there don't want the police looking round too much. Also, remember in Guinea people are still executed for murder," Abdul said.

"The flooded river would have stopped people coming from the direction of Matakourou without some kind of boat," Howard said.

"Yes, I've questioned the people in the villages, old and new, and they say there weren't any strangers staying here during the weekend. Also they say Tamba came back around nine o' clock and walked down the path to the river. He told them he was looking for Leila."

"But why didn't he tell you that? And why did he not go on his motorcyle?"

"I'll wait for the report from Beyla and then question him again," Abdul said.

"I'll get statements from the manager, Mrs. Taylor and the other expatriates," Howard said. Is everything Okay here now?"

"Yes. No one seems too concerned that Buzzard died. Obviously, we have to get the inquiry finished."

"I'm off now, but will see you tomorrow," Howard said. 'I've thought of something while I was away. We should see if anything fell into the pit. We could clean it out and wash it through a sieve."

"Sounds like a good idea. Why don't you do it with some of the new Security men we've recruited?" Abdul suggested. "We can start to find out what they're like. I don't think it's correct to leave them to work on their own too much."

"I will."

CHAPTER 10

HOWARD DROVE HIS Landrover up to his cabin, parked it on its stand, pulled out his bag, unlocked the door and went inside. It was hot and stuffy, inside so he opened two of the windows. He was glad to be back. He sat down at the table and switched on his cassette player. He decided if he returned to Banam after leave in England, he would buy a television set with a VCR player. If Jean got a video camera she could send him tapes from England and also copy programmes from her television. He could buy the equipment from the company store at a discounted price. As he was getting a bonus for living out here, he could pay out of that.

After awhile he became bored and decided to go and see the manager. He took a notebook from a shelf and walked down to Bob Taylor's office.

Bob was sitting at his desk, reading a report from Banbury.

"You're not too busy are you, Bob?" he asked.

"Yes, I am. But I'm always looking for an excuse to stop reading these reports. I can do with a break. What can I do for you?"

"I'm trying to tie up the loose ends on this Buzzard business. When you and Angeline left me that evening, you did come straight home.—Didn't you?"

"Yes. Angeline was tired. So, after some cheese on toast, we went to bed."

"You don't mind if I talk to Angeline, do you?"

"Of course not. She'll tell you the same thing."

"Well, thanks. Would you like to be there when I talk to her?"

"Not at all. She's up at the house now. What's the latest news on the Buzzard death?"

"We're just waiting for a report from the Guinea police. That should end it. Also, I've decided to clean out the pit to see if there was anything in it. You've no objection? Have you?"

"Of course not. Go ahead."

Howard walked out of the office up the road to the manager's house. He knocked on the door. "Anyone in?"

A young Guinean girl about sixteen years old opened the door.

"Come in, Mr Evans. Mrs. Taylor is in the lounge." She led the way into the lounge where Angeline was sitting in an armchair.

"Okay Marie," Angeline said, "Just finish the ironing and you can go for the day."

"Thank you, Mrs. Taylor. But what about dinner?"

"I can manage. Everything's ready. Take the your food from the fridge."

The girl disappeared into the kitchen.

"Her father has asked me to train her to cook, do ironing, housework and that kind of thing. I think he thinks it will make her more marriageable. Anyway, what can I do for you?"

"Angeline, Bob said you and he came home, ate supper and went to bed last Sunday and you didn't go anywhere else?"

"That's right."

"My next question is a little more personal."

"I won't be annoyed. I think I know what you're going to ask."

"I noticed at your birthday party you were upset when Buzzard said something about your mother. Why were you so scared of what he might say?"

"My dislike of Buzzard had nothing to do with his death. I can assure you that neither Bob nor I had any reason to kill him, if that's what you want to know."

"I'm only trying to antipate what might be asked at the inquest in England. Was it anything he found out when he was in the police force? Remember I have heard of his reputation."

As though deciding if she should trust him, Angeline looked at Howard.

"Anything you tell me will be confidential unless it has anything to do with Buzzard's death."

"Well, I suppose it must be in Police Records. Buzzard was trying to backmail me."

"But why? What did he know about you?"

"You know what a bastard he could be. He wanted to sleep with me and knew something about my mother. When she was very young, she'd been convicted of petty theft, shoplifting and other minor crimes. She told me it was because she got into a bad crowd who used to smoke pot and that kind of thing. Luckily, she was only given probation and realized how stupid she'd been. So, she worked hard and turned her life around. After a few years, she had enough money to rent a newpaper shop in Banbury. But Buzzard must have heard of the Witney crowd and I look just like my mother. When I mentioned my mother had lived in Witney; Buzzard must have realized I was her daughter. I decided Bob would know how to deal with it if I had to tell him and told Buzzard I wouldn't be blackmailed. That's why he was just trying to cause trouble."

"Okay. Angeline. It's won't go any further."

"Would you like a cup of tea?"

"Yes, please."

Angeline went into the kitchen and a few minutes later, came back with a tray containing tea things and biscuits. After drinking the tea and eating two biscuits, Howard said, "Goodbye," and walked back to his house.

He ate a supper of melted cheese and bacon on toast, took a shower and went to bed.

CHAPTER 11

THE NEXT MORNING, Thursday, Howard got to the office early. He decided to talk to Tom Gough, the Prospecting Supervisor as well as Jeffrey Ellis. He started at the Prospecting Washsite down the hill, past the offices, on the road to the new river bridge.

The washsite was the sampling plant for the area and was portable like the plant The main section, with the Hartz jigs and sorting office, was on a chassis and had rubber-tyred wheels. It could be towed by a tractor.

The loading bay was made of steel sheets. Howard saw Tom Gough here. He was an overweight man, 5'9" tall and looked about sixty years old. His Security dossier said he had a drinking problem. He had an unkempt beard and was sweating profusely.

"You haven't met my homologue, Momoh, have you?" he asked.

The three men shook hands and Momoh went into the aluminium-roofed office.

"Good morning, Howard. What can we do for you?" Tom asked.

"Well, you can show me the washsite and afterwards, I'd like to ask you a few questions about last Sunday."

"Okay. As you can see, it's a simple set-up. The gravel normally arrives in trailors, towed by tractors. We empty the trailor in the bay and wash it with a hose into the sizing trommel underneath. We're on a small hill, so it's gravity fed."

"How are the samples dug?"

"In the old days, they were dug by hand. But these days, labour is more expensive and the samples are dug using a Poclain hydraulic excavator. It's very efficient. I supervise the digging and the washing on alternate days. Every sample is given a number and has a ticket, so we don't make mistakes. Everything is recorded in the log book and in the daily return."

"How do you decide where to dig?"

"I don't. We get a map from the Prospecting Department in Matakourou with the pit sites marked. It's done on a grid system. If we find enough diamonds in an area, it becomes a future mining block. We're still marking out blocks here whereas the blocks in Matakourou have been designated."

"So, if you had a Prospecting map, you could tell which are the profitable areas?"

"Yes. That's one of the problems and the reason why we try and limit the accessibility of the maps."

"I can see this rotating washer has different screen sizes and a milk churn underneath to collect the gravel."

"That's right. They're called trommels. I believe it's Afrikaans for a drum. This large size is hand sorted, wheeled away in wheelbarrows and then used around the houses."

"So, obviously you have electricity?"

"Yes. We have our own generator in that shed over there. Again, it's mobile. Remember, we're self supporting. The churns are brought here." He led the way into the Hartz jig section off the Sorting Office.

"The churns are hoisted up to the platform above the jigs and tipped into the machine hoppers. When the gravel is very dry, we use a small water hose to feed the gravel into the machine. Otherwise, it is gravity fed. The gravel falls into the centre of the tray. The up and down motion causes the light materials to float over the edges of the tray and the heavier materials to stay in the centre of the tray. The hutch underneath has water in it and there's a outlet that is opened when the process is finished. If there is any doubt about the effectiveness of the jigging, we reload the hoppers and re-jig. Anyway, let's show you a few trays."

They went into the sorting office where Momoh was waiting. It was fenced in with expanded meta screens. There was a large metal table, extending between the jig area and the sorting office. This had an opening over it that could be closed. The Guinean operator in the jigging section lifted out a filled jig tray, brought it to the metal table, fitted a wooden board over the gravel, reversed it and left it for Tom and the homologue to examine. There were no diamonds in the sample, but minerals such as illeminite, corundum and garnet were found and extracted."

"What happens when you get diamonds?" Howard asked.

"We put them in a container that goes into a packet and then into the safe. When the plant sends their diamonds to Matakourou, we add ours."

Eventually, two small diamonds were extracted from the sample, measured in millimetres, weighed and recorded in the log book and daily sheet. They were then locked in the safe.

"We'll take a break for about fifteen minutes, Momoh," Tom said.

"That's fine with me. I'm going up to the camp."

"Let's go outside,." Tom said.

They went outside and sat on two folding canvas chairs.

"Fire away," Tom said. "What do you want to know?

"Well what happened last Sunday? Remember, we're really only concerned with what happened after nine p.m."

"I was a bit hung over by that time. I started drinking in the morning and carried on into the evening. I missed dinner and went to bed early. But I did walk down to the Washsite after the rain to see if everything was alright. But I didn't see the watchman there. Afterwards, I returned to bed. I was drinking with Jeffrey Ellis most of the time."

"You didn't see anyone around after nine o' clock."

"No. But it was dark out there at that time. I took a flashlight."

"That seems Okay. If I think of anything else, I'll contact you." Howard wrote down some of the details in his notebook, put it in the pocket of his khaki jacket and walked away. He decided to see Jeffrey Ellis to see what he would say. He found him in the club kitchen making a pot of tea.

"Would you like a cup?" he asked Howard. "I've made some scones, as well. We can sit in the baffa outside. Strawberry jam sound Okay with the scones."

"Yes, There's a cafe in Banbury which is famous for it scones."

"Though I say it myself, mine aren't bad."

The men sat outside, drinking tea and eating scones. It was so peaceful and comfortable, Howard didn't want to ask questions but eventually he started. "You know I have to ask everyone where they were Sunday night? Obviously, in an independent state like Guinea I don't have any legal standing. But I've been asked to find out what I can and help the Guineans to determine how Mark Buzzard died."

"I don't mind answering a few questions."

"Tom Gough says you were drinking with him up until the evening."

"That's right. He was so drunk, he went to bed before dinner. But I had to make sure the evening meal was ready, so I didn't drink too much. Afterwards, Bob Taylor and me watched a French film someone had brought back from Paris. Remember, the VCR's work on the PAL system here. The film was pretty hot. Abdul Kourouma came in later on to see if his wife was back but he didn't stay. I don't think it was his kind of film. About ten o' clock, there was nobody here so I locked up and went to my house. "

"So you didn't notice anyone hanging around the place, even when you were watching the video?"

"Definity not. Remember, it rained for most of the evening."

"Thanks for your cooperation, Mr. Ellis."

It was lunchtime, so Howard walked back to his house and ate lunch.

After lunch he walked down to the Security Office to discuss his interviews with Abdul Kourouma. He told Abdul what he had been told by Tom Gough and Jeffrey Ellis.

"I wouldn't suspect either of them," Abdu said, with a smile. "Tom is another customer of Leila, the assistant witchdoctor's wife, though he may not pay her in cash. And, we suspect Jeffrey Ellis is a little too fond of some of the local youths."

"You don't seem too upset about Jeffrey?" Howard said.

"Mr. Evans, we need industry here in Guinea. This mine here could help raise our standard of living. If Ellis is discreet and doesn't start playing around with children, we'll turn a blind eye to it. It's like Leila. Prostitution is strictly prohited in Guinea. But where in the world have we been able to stop it? They're very strict in Conakry. It is illegal for an expatriate who is by himself to take a Guinean women to a restaurant in Conakry."

"What have you discovered about Tamba?"

"I've received a report from the police in Beyla that says he contacted a diamond buyer from Liberia at the weekend. I'm going to Conakry tomorrow on the company plane to talk to the Interior Ministry and Mines Department about the case. If you like, you could have a pot luck dinner with Jeanine and me tonight and we could discuss the case further."

"I'd like that. What time?"

"Come about six o' clock. We can watch television and have a drink before the meal. I'm a Muslim. But, like most military men, I don't abstain from acohol. It may be because I have a French wife."

"See you then."

Howard spent the afternoon driving around the area to see that everything looked normal. He didn't spot anything unusual and was quite happy when he arrived home.

He showered and changed into slacks and a dress shirt for his dinner at the Kouroumas. He wasn't quite sure what to expect. He'd obtained a bottle of French Beaujolais wine from the Provision Store. Howard bought the wine because he reasoned he must have a bigger dollar food allowance than the Kouroumas.

He was pleased to be having dinner with Abdul and Jeanine because he hoped the Security Department here might get the kind of camaraderie he had seen in the Banbury Police.

The Kourouma's house was large. Abdul had added two wings to the original container. Abdul met Howard in the screened in courtyard. "Jeanine's showing the maid how to do the cooking."

"It smells good," Howard said. "We can sit out here and watch a French video news tape." He switched on the television set. "What would you like to drink?"

"A beer, please."

Abdul went and came back with two Stella Artois beers." They sat there drinking their beers and watching the video.

"I've brought a bottle of Beaujolais."

"Jeanine likes Beaujolais. Thanks." Abdul took the bottle into the kitchen.

Jeanine and the maid came out of the kitchen, carrying a table that they put at one side of the courtyard. Jeanine was wearing a light, lemon coloured short dress which emphasized her slim figure. The maid set the table for dinner.

The dinner was very good and highly seasoned. Howard was pleased when Abdul mentioned his love of French literature and the poems of Baudelaire.

"I studied French at school in Fishguard. We had to read 'Les Miserables,' by Victor Hugo. I still remember the trials and tribulations of Jean Valjean and his yellow card. I think the inspector's name was Javert, or something like that," Howard said.

"Yes. Of course, we had to study all the French authors. One of my favourites is Baudelaire and his 'Les Fleurs du Mal.' Abdul quoted one long passage from the poem. Howard was quite impressed.

Jeanine told Howard how she first met Abdul. She was teaching languages at a Lycee in Paris at the time. One of her languages was Russian and she took a summer course in Moscow that Abdul attended. He was doing a course with the Soviet Russian Army.

"I've lived in Guinea for about five years now. Before we came here, we lived in Conakry and I taught there. I hope that they'll start a school here and I can teach again."

Howard told the story about how he had met Jean, his wife. She had parked her car on the Horsefair in Banbury and locked the keys inside. He had helped her unlock it and arranged to meet her later at the Whately Hotel. "We got married a year later."

Jeanine said, "goodnight" to Howard and went into the kitchen.

Howard and Abdul sat outside, discussing Buzzard's death.

"The main suspect must be Tamba. It seems as though he and Buzzard had some kind of argument and Tamba hit him. It has to be something to do with diamonds because Tamba went down south to meet a dealer," Abdul said.

"That's why I have to go to Conakry. They'll arrange to send an examining judge to question Tamba."

"But there are other people who could have encountered Buzzard on Sunday. Tom Gough said he walked down to the Washsite. That's not too far from where Buzzard was found."

"We'll have to see what they decide in Conakry,." Abdul reiterated. "I'll see you when I come back. I have to leave early tomorrow morning."

Howard said "Goodnight" and went to his house.

CHAPTER 12

O N SATURDAY, HOWARD awoke early, around six am, just as it was getting light. Tthe sound of Abdul's Landrover going down the road toward the river, had awakened him. The river was low enough to ford now.

After showering and dressing, he decided to take a walk up the hills above his house. It was cool and there was a breeze blowing tranversely across the hill. He left his house and was walking along below the houses when he noticed Mohamed, the young boy he had taken to Matakourou, coming toward him.

"Morning, Mohamed. You're up early?"

"Yes, Mr. Evans. I'm going to clean the club before I go to out to our farm. I've just got the keys from Mr. Ellis."

Howard thought it was odd that he came so early on Saturday. But he carried on until he reached the road going up the hill.

The walk invigorated him and he was happy when he went back to his house for breakfast. He cooked eggs and bacon and made himself a carafe of coffee.

He walked down to the Security Office, said "Good morning," to the radio operator and asked, "Any messages?"

"Nothing at all."

About 7.30 am, Jeanine passed the office and he went outside. She was wearing running shoes, shorts and a tee-shirt.

"You going out to the plant?" he asked.

"Yes. Like to come?"

"Yes. As long as you don't go too fast."

They jogged out to the plant in about thirty minutes, without talking. The plant was operating in its usual noisy, manner with dust and water everywhere. They walked into the office.

Dan Spring was in charge today. "Any problems Dan?" Howard asked.

"No. Everything's going well."

"Well, I'd better get back to the plant, See you later Jeanine."

"Yes. I'll see you at the party tonight."

"I almost forgot that."

Howard took a slow, comfortable walk back to the Security Post and his office.

As he wasn't too busy, he decided to clean out the material from the pit where he had found Buzzard. He went to see Tom Gough in the Washsite. After collecting a rope, bucket, shovel and shaker, he returned to his office. The shaker was a wooden hoop with chicken mesh stretched over it. He took his office clerk and another Security man down the path to the old pit. The men climbed down into it and dug out the soft soil from the bottom. This was placed in the bucket. Howard didn't expect to find anything, but he'd had the idea and decided to do it.

When he returned to the Washsite and washed the sand, gravel and soil through he shaker, he was surprised to find some objects on the screen of the shaker. He found a small rusty penknife and a man's signet ring. When he cleaned up the penknife, he found the initials RHA engraved on the side. But the gold signet ring, plain except for a small garnet, yielded no clues to its origin. He showed Tom Gough and Momoh what he had found.

"As it doesn't contain diamonds, you may as well take them away. Do you agree Momoh? I notice it doesn't have hallmarks, so presumably must have been made locally?"

"Yes. It doesn't look valuable. If you don't take them now, there'll be arguments for days about what to do with them. Think of the paperwork we'll have to do."

"Yes," Howard said. "I'll tell Bob Taylor and Abdul Kourouma when I see them."

Tom gave him a small plastic box to put them in, but he couldn't find either Bob or Abdul.

He spent the rest of the morning doing paperwork in his office.

At lunchtime, he went to the club for companionship and a few drinks. Most of the male members of the camp were there. Jeanine came in later and sat at Howard's table. He learned from Jeffrey Ellis that the dinner would commence at 6:30 pm and would be buffet style. He left the club baffa at two o' clock, went back to his house, had a bread and cheese sandwich with a beer and spent the rest of the afternoon sleeping in a chair on his verandah.

Howard awoke about four o'clock. He had a stiff neck, dishevelled clothes and felt dry and thirsty. He went inside the house, that was stinking hot and opened all the windows. switched on the fan and took off all his clothes. He slumped into the single armchair, with its wooden arms and khaki cotton cushions. For a few minutes, it was like being in a turkish bath and he enjoyed the sensation of sweating profusely, even though he knew he was soaking the cushions. The sight of Jeanine walking past his house caused him to jump rapidly into the shower room.

After his shower, he changed into long trousers and a clean, white cotton shirt. His laundry was always very well done and his shirts looked as though they could have been used for advertisements for soap powders. The laundry was done, the traditional way using handmade soap by some of the village women employed by DIASA. The smell of the laundry always reminded Howard of his uncles in the Gwaun valley who must have used similar unscented soaps. Afterward, he made some tea and sat in the damp armchair, reading a paperback novel and drinking his tea.

By six o' clock, he was bored and ready for the evening's entertainment. When he saw Jeanine go past the house, he followed her down to the club. There were several people in the outside bar. Tom Gough and Bob Taylor were leaning on the bar and looked as though they had been there all afternoon.

"Tom's told me you found a knife and ring in the Buzzard pit," Bob said.

"Yes. Though there's no indication who they belonged to, except the knife has the initials RHA on it. I'd like to put them in your safe."

"Bring them along on Monday. There's no hurry. They must have been there for years."

The Guinean barman served Jeanine with the glass of white wine she ordered and brought Howard the Stella Artois beer he ordered. Howard took it to one of the tables and sat on one of the benches which circled the baffa inside the walls. He surveyed this curious thatched large circular building, with its small walls and open sides. It made him feel he was in tropical Africa. Jeanine stood at the barm talking to Bob Taylor and Tom Gough. When Dan Spring walked in, they went and sat at a table by themselves.

A few minutes later, Jeffrey Ellis walked in.

"Dinner's ready when you want it," he said. "I hope everyone likes peppered chicken. But there is a salad and I'll cook fish for anyone who doesn't like the chicken."

No one refused the chicken that was promptly placed on a central table at seven o' clock.

After the meal Jeanine was persuaded to sing some of her French songs. Dan Spring companied her on his guitar. Afterwards, they sat talking to each other in the outside bar.

Later, the men watched one of the videos they had in the inside room. It was a copy of "Zulu," starring Michael Caine. Howard resolved to bring back some videos when he came from leave. The men then joined Dan and Jeanine at the outside bar.

The group started splitting up at eleven o' clock and going home.

"Don't forget the picnic tomorrow," Jeffrey Ellis said. "Remember, a lot of people are coming from Matakourou so we want to put on a good show. We need volunteers to start the thing off a twelve o' clock. I've had the grass cut and the barbeques are set up. So we are ready."

Howard, Jeanine, Dan and Bob volunteered to be there the next day. Tom Gough was too drunk to say anything and was helped to his house by Bob Taylor.

Howard walked up the hill to his house and went to bed. One of his last thoughts before going to sleep was how people like Tom Gough could have done this for so many years.

CHAPTER 13

A S USUAL, HE awoke early the next morning and went for a walk up the hill. He met Mohamed walking along the road, but did not say anything. He carried on up the road going to the top of the hill. He was two hundred yards up the road when he looked back and saw a slight figure coming out of the back door of the Taylor's house. He couldn't see who it was, but by the clothes he knew it was a young girl. She continued along the road into the village.

After his walk up the hill and testing the radio there, he returned to his house. He had breakfast and then decided to start to work on a garden. This was the first time he had lived in a hot country, so he wished to try and grow tropical fruits like bananas, pineapples, paw paws, oranges and lemons. His idea was to use the flat, cleared area outside the back of the house for the bananas, pineapples and things like peppers. He could grow the citrus fruit on a cleared area up the hill. Afterwards, if he was still enthusiastic, he would put flowers like bourganvilleas, lilies and flowering shrubs in front of the house. He started off with vigour, using a small shovel to bring soil from the hill to make small raised beds. In three hours, he had finished two beds and decided it was time to stop.

Aat eleven11 o' clock, he walked into the house, took a Coca Cola from the refrigerator and drank it. He showered and changed into a clean pair of shorts and a clean khaki shirt. Afterwards, he drove down to the club.

"Anything I can take out to the picnic site?" he asked.

"Well, you can take these metal dustbins out there. We'll fill them with ice and beer and use them first. They make very efficient coolers," Jeffrey Ellis answered.

Howard loaded the dustbins into his Landrover and drove out to the picnic site. This was about a mile from the bridge under construction where the river was shallow and fordable. It was large, flat, sandy site that had been partially cleared of vegetation. There were some small, distorted trees away from the river. Thatched shelters had been constructed in case of rain. There was a wickerwork screen put up as a urinal and two outhouses with pits underneath. These would be filled in after the picnic.

Some of his security men were already there, setting up the barbeques and filling them with charcoal. Howard knew these jobs were very popular because the men were paid extra and they were given meals and the leftover food and drinks to take home.

Jeffrey Ellis arrived at twelve o' clock with a lorry full of iceboxes, refrigerators and a small generator. These were unloaded and put under one of the shelters. The generator was started and the iceboxes and refrigerators plugged in.

People started arriving from Matakourou. They left their vehicles on the Matakourou side of the river, in case the water level rose and it was difficult to cross over.

Eventually, fourteen people arrived from Matakourou. One of the young plant engineers brought his wife and two young children. They all waded across the river and selected their shaded shelter to sit beneath. Most were wearing swimsuits that they had changed into, or were wearing under their clothes which they removed.

The Banam people arrived in Landrovers and selected their places. Howard noticed Jeanine because she was wearing a skimpy bikini that emphasized her slim figure and bronzed colouring. Dan Spring was driving the Landrover that also contained Francoise and her brother, Mohamed. Francoise was wearing a bikini which Jeanine had given her. It was a bright crimson colour showing she was developing into a shapely young woman. Howard realized she wasn't as young as he had thought and noticed how some of the men were admiring her figure. Even Bob Taylor was giving her surreptitious glances.

Jeffrey Ellis had brought a CD player and loud speakers, and he played popular music all afternoon. The barbeque went well and everyone helped themselves to the hamburgers, sausages and chicken. A table was set up with complementary food with the barbeque. Afterwards, there was icecream and other sweets, followed by tea and coffee. A lot of the men, however, like Tom Gough, just drank beer. Howard noticed he augmented the beer with liquid from a shiny whiskey flask that he used quite frequently. He noticed him because he had the flask that looked as though it was made of siver, inconspicuously, in an old army water bottle sling. He didn't offer it to anyone else. Also he drank rather secretly, like a marooned sailor on a desert island hoarding his supplies. Tom was not a good mixer at a party, anytime. He left early before he got too drunk.

After the meal, a lot of the younger people and the children played games. There was soccer and volley balls and the river to play with.

About three o' clock, a lorry arrived from Banam with a group of devil dancers to entertain the visitors. These masked and cloaked figures looked scary and the two children stayed close to their parents. Howard was intrigued by them. They were dressed in black robes, covered with raffia stalks. A wooden mask covered the face. A group of musicians with local instruments accompanied the dancers. The dancing consisted of whirling circular movements which were repeated. The main devil was beaten by other devils who used leather whips. Howard thought he recognized the main devil as Tamba, the truck driver. He was also known as Suluku, the hyena, of his distorted face. Though Howard wasn't sure because of the mask.

After the entertainment had finished, one of the visitors started a fund with local money and dollars to reward the dancers. Howard was sure they would also be paid by Ellis. They were invited to help themselves to the food and soft drinks. Afterwards they went home in the lorry.

About 4:30 pm, the Matakourou visitors left. They wanted to arrive home before it got dark. The Banam group stayed until 6:00 pm, and finished off most of the food before they left. The rest would be delivered to the village by the security men.

Howard collected up his now empty dustbins to take to the clubhouse store. After unloading there he went to the outside bar where the other men were. He stayed until the place closed about nine pm. He then drove up to his house and went to bed.

CHAPTER 14

*H*OWARD AWOKE EARLY the next morning at six am. He wondered why, until suddenly remembering he was going to escort a shipment of concentrate to Matakourou. He ate a hasty breakfast of cornflakes and tea. Then, he drove out to the plant and arrived before seven am. Dan Spring and a Guinean Security man were already there supervising the loading of milk churns onto a flatbed lorry.

"Morning Howard, You ready?"

"Yes. What do I have to do?"

"Well, Count the cans and check that the seal number agree with the delivery note. Then, you get in your Landrover and follow the lorry to the Separator House in Matakourou. It's the small building next to the new plant. Just make sure the lorry gets there. Take the radio but remember it won't operate in some places. This Guinean guard will go with the lorry. The other will go with you. They both have AK47's, so you should be quite safe."

Howard checked the seal numbers and they all agreed with the waybill's numbers.

"They're correct," he said to Dan.

"Okay. Just follow the lorry to Matakourou. The lorry will have to ford the river because of its weight. Just make sure you get a receipt for the correct number of cans. You can return immediately after you emptied the lorry. It can return by itself. But you might like to see how they recover the diamonds."

"Yes, I'll stay and see how its done and come back after lunch."

"I've radioed Matakourou. The password today is 'Ceres'. It changes everyday."

Howard returned to his Landrover with the security man. He was surprised to see Tamba Suluku getting ready to drive his truck out to the gravel loading cut. But, he was more concerned with getting the concentrate lorry to Matakouou. As it was a dry day and the river level was low enough to ford, the trip was easy.

The lorry drove directly to the Separator House, a small building next to the Treatment Plant.

The twenty cans were unloaded onto a concrete platfrom, lifted by an electric hoist and pulled into the building through a small door onto a expanded steel deck. There was a small door on the ground floor and Howard was allowed to enter, while the guard stayed outside with the vehicle.

Howard climbed up some steel stairs to where the cans had been unloaded. He noticed the labourers had sleeveless uniforms without pockets held together with tapes, not buttons. The building did not have windows, though it was very well lit with blazing lights. There was an expatriate supervisor and several Guinean Security personnel overseeing the operations inside. The expatriate introduced himself and said, "Let's tell you a bit about the process. Basically, nothing that comes in here is thrown away. It's all ground up in ball or rod mills. Firstly, it goes into the hopper here, over the vanner, into baskets underneath. The vanner contains heated grease, so it is degreased in a solvent, washed in a soapy rinse, dried in an oven and then sorted. We do have a new machine, a sortex, that sorts electronically, but we can also sort by hand in the little offices I'll show you later. But lets start."

He emptied the can into the hopper. The produce travelled along a curved, greased conveyor belt that had water jets directed across it. The diamonds and heavy materials stuck to the belt and were scraped off at the bottom into a basket. The lighter materials were washed off and finished up in ball or rod mills.

Howard and the supervisor went to the bottom of the Vanner to see the operation in progress. The basket at the bottom was dipped into vats for the various treatments. First, it went into a vat with a solvent to remove the grease. Then, it was washed to remove the solvent. Howard noticed the packets of a popular soap detergent nearby. "We do this so we don't blow ourselves up! The oven is very hot but dries very quickly."

While they were waiting for the basket to dry, the supervisor showed Howard how they hand sorted. "The sorter sits outside this booth, with one arm inside, enveloped in a rubber glove. A security man sits on the other side and watches through the window. The sorter picks up the diamond, using tweezers, and puts them in a locked container. This goes on until the cans are finished. You'll notice we have sample tickets, so we know where the gravel came from. There's a terrific amount of paperwork that goes with the diamonds to Conakry. The diamonds are normally put into large manilla envelopes for transportation."

"What about the Sortex machine?"

"A laser beam picks out the diamonds from the other concentrate and an air jet blows them into a locked container, while the rest of the concentrate goes into a ball mill. Obviously, we prefer the Sortex because we don't have to supervise so closely. But we're not too clued up about its maintenance. We've just had an expert from South Africa fixing it. I'll show you how it works with this basket."

Howard spent the rest of the morning in the Separator House, seeing the vaious operations. Sean MacVeigh came in while he was there and told him he could have lunch at the Rest House.

About twelve o' clock, Howard drove along to the Rest House. He sat reading in the lounge until lunch was called at 12.30pm. He realized why he had been offered lunch in the Rest House when he saw the other guest for lunch. It was the technician from South Africa.

"I'm Howard Evans," Howard introduced himself. "I work for the Security Department at Banam up the valley."

"I'm Charlie Forbes. I've been here since yesterday working on the two Sortex machines. I live in South Africa, but was born in Britain and luckily have a British passport."

"Why's that?"

"You can't travel in a lot of African countries with a South African passport. I had to go to London to get here."

"It must have been expensive for DIASA?"

"Yes. I think so. Especially as the machines didn't need much maintenance. The main trouble that was the mirrors needed cleaning."

"You must have an interesting life, travelling from one country to another?"

"Yes. I'm going to Angola after this."

"But, doesn't the Angolan government suspect you come from South Africa?"

"They almost certainly know, but where else would you get an expert on a machine mainly used in South Africa?"

The lunch was very good. At one o' clock, Howard excused himself, drove to the Provision Store for supplies and returned to Banam. There were no problems on the way. He drove to the Security Department office. Abdul Kourouma had come back from Conakry and was in his small office at the end of the building.

"How did the trip go?" Howard asked.

"A judge is coming up to question Tamba and anyone else he wants to see. He should be here next week. I've also brought a letter from Pierrre Beauregard. It's about the inquest in Oxford at the end of November. I know because we're both going. Come to dinner tonight and we'll talk about it then. 6:30 sound Okay?"

"Yes, but I do seem to be imposing on you?"

"No. I'm just making sure you'll look after us in England."

"Yes. That's true. You could even stay with us, if you like."

"We'll see. It might be more convenient for us to stay in Oxford. But let's talk about it tonight. I want to sort out these reports from Conakry."

"Okay. Did Jeanine tell you what I found in the Buzzard pit?"

"Yes. Could you bring them along tonight?"

"Yes. I will."

Howard walked to his office at the other end of the building. After his conversation with Abdul, he was a little restless so he decided to take a trip out to the plant. But first, he decided he had to show Bob Taylor the ring and knife he had found in the Buzzard pit. He walked over to his office.

Bob Taylor was sitting at his desk, going through some reports.

"Bob, on Saturday, I washed some material from the pit where we found Buzzard and found these." Howard produced the ring and knife he had found and put them on the table.

"I suppose they could have been washed in from anywhere?"

"That's true, but the knife has the initials RHA on it," Howard said. He was amazed Bob didn't seem to think it was an important find.

"I'll lock them in the safe until I find out what Banbury wants to do about them? Is there anything else?"

"No!" Howard replied and left.

He spent the rest of the morning at the plant. As usual, things were normal and gravel was being processed as it arrived at the plant. He drove out to the loading site and watched the loading for some time. Then, he drove around the area looking for illegal diggings. Again he drew a blank. At four o' clock, he finished work and drove back the Security Post. He went and looked at the composite houses being constructed for his security personnel. They were using a mold to make the blocks out of clay and cement, and the foreman was doing the construction efficiently. He realized he could not help, so went back to see if the radio operator had any messages for him. There were no messages from the radio operator and Abdul had gone home, so he went up to his house.

He sat on his verandah, writing a letter to his wife and drinking a cold beer until he decided to get ready for his dinner with the Kourouma's. He remembered he had not read the letter from Banbury. As Abdul had said, it gave the date; end of November for the inquest on Buzzard. When he had finished his letter, he showered and dressed in long trousers for his dinner engagement.

When he arrived at the Kourouma's house next door, he found there were other guests. The Taylor's and Dan Spring were sitting in the courtyard with Abdul.

"What would you like to drink?" Abdul inquired.

"Beer, please, Abdul. I'm afraid I couldn't bring those things I found in the pit because Bob has locked them away in his safe."

"There's no problem. He did show them to me."

Abdul went away and returned with the Stella Artois beer he knew Howard liked. This was one of the things Howard was beginning to like about Africans. They always remembered your likes and dislikes.

Conversation was brisk, with Abdul doing most of the talking. Howard realized he had had an interesting time in Conakry.

"I found out something interesting when I went to the Ministry of Mines at the weekend. There's an old mine about 60 miles from here which was run by the British before the war. When France surrendered to Germany in 1940, the young manager tried to take the diamond production to Sierra Leone. But he never arrived. He was found dead somewhere near here. They think he was murdered by bandits. He's buried near the old plant down in the valley. A biscuit tin containing diamonds was recovered from the manager's backpack. The theory is the thieves were disturbed when they were robbing him and they didn't get away with any of the diamonds."

"What happened to the murderers?" Bob asked.

"They were executed by the French. It was wartime so it would have been quick. The British came back after the war. When De Gualle withdrew the French technicians, they left. De Gaulle was annoyed because Sekou Torre wouldn't join his French Commonwealth. Later the Russians ran the diamond mines. A lot of the locals think there were more diamonds they were hidden by the murderers and haven't been found. That's why there are so many holes dug along the old path from the river."

"That's very interesting," Howard said. "Because I found a knife inscribed RHA and a signet ring with a garnet set in it in the old pit where Buzzard was found."

This started a conversation about the old mine and the lost diamonds.

"I'd like to visit the old mine," Howard said. "What's there now?."

"Apparantly, the clerk from the British days still lives there. He worked for the Russians when they ran it. Remember, Russia has a huge diamond industry in Siberia. They made a lot of money here. Except for the clerk and his family, nobody lives there now. Occasionally, some illicit diggers dig, but the police soon get wind of it and chase them out. There's an agricultural village six miles away. If we took tents and supplies, we could stay there. The French built a very sophisicated water pumping station there for irrigation, so it has electricity as well. I'd like to see that."

"So, we could go there?" Dan Spring asked.

"Certainly. You know how we like to show off something that's working well. Let's go next weekend. I'll make the necessary arrangements." Abdul said.

"I'd like to go," Dan said.

"I can't go because I'm too busy. But I'm sure Angeline would like to go,." Bob Taylor said.

"I'd love to go," Angeline said. "It sounds interesting."

"Jeanine will like to come," Abdul said.

"What was that about me?" Jeanine said coming from the kitchen.

"I said you'd like to visit the old mine next Saturday. We could go for the weekend."

"Yes, certainly. I'd love to go. If we take Francoise, she can help with the meals. I'll ask her."

"We'll leave at one o' clock on Saturday. The road will almost certainly be bad so I'd like to arrive before dark. We'll take my motorcycle to scout the road. I know some of the bridges are bad, but people still use them or ford the rivers. I'll send a message to the clerk, Abdul Kourouma, to let the villagers know we're coming. I believe he's some distant relative of mine."

Abdul said.

"Yes. You can take two Landrovers, and we have tents and sleeping bags at the office,"

Bob Taylor said.

"I came to say dinner is ready," Jeanine said. "I'm teaching Francoise to cook, so we'd better sit down."

"I've brought a bottle of Beaujolais,." Howard said. "Your favourite."

"We've invited the right people tonight, Abdul. We've enough drinks for a Christmas party. Everybody brought something French," Jeanine said. "Let's eat."

Everyone sat down at the table. Jeanine went into the house and came out carrying some dishes of food. Francoise followed with some more dishes.

The guests all greeted Francoise. She looked very young and serious in a plain blue dress.

"Good evening, everybody,." she said.

She went to the kitchen and came back with two bottles of wine. She poured out a glass and handed it to Jeanine. Jeanine poured out a glass for each person.

"We're having salad instead of soup, Francoise. Just come back for the plates. Then, serve the meringue pie followed by coffee. If there are any problems, just call me," Jeanine said.

The meal was very well cooked and efficiently served.

Afterwards, sitting in a comfortable armchair drinking brandy, Howard thought about what a pleasant and friendly evening it had been. At midnight, he said, "goodnight" and walked back to his house.

CHAPTER 15

THE WEEK PASSED quite quickly. Howard wanted to recruit a mobile force of twenty men who could cover the whole lease area. They would be recruited when their houses were finished. His present force was made up of Guinean army personnel and five men recruited by the former Security Officer. At present, the emphasis was on plant and mining security. He was determined to make sure things were run properly and there were no security lapses. He checked up on the plant, Prospecting Washsite and gravel loading sites daily. He didn't notice any irregularities.

He kept an eye on the village to make sure there were only DIASA workers, or family members living there. For the rest of the week, he took his five men out to patrol the lease area of the company. He didn't have anything to report on his weekly Situation Reports sent to Matakourou.

On Thursday, Sean McVeigh spent several hours with him visiting the plant and the mining areas.

"I think it would a good idea to recruit another ten security men to start as soon as possible. We still don't cover enough of the lease area. The illegals could be digging in a lot of the more remote areas. Get them to build temporary posts until we can finish permanent ones. I suggest a good place to start would be near that border bridge going down to the old mine."

He didn't say too much for the rest of his visit. He brought a sandwich lunch with him which he ate in the office. Howard wondered if he had upset him, or if he had information that made it seem as though Howard wasn't doing his job properly. Sean left for Matakourou at three o' clock.

When he finished work on Saturday, Howard hurried to his house and ate a ham sandwich washed down with a beer. He was excited about his trip to the old mine because he wanted to see more of Guinea and its population. He quckly assembled his clothes for the weekend put them into a leather bag and tranferred them to his Landrover with the sleeping bags, cooking utensils and the tent. He then waited inside. At 12:20 pm, Angeline Taylor walked up to the house and he opened the door to let her in. She looked cool in a pair of yellow shorts and a blue T shirt.

"Ready?" he asked. He took her bag and put it in the Landrover.

"Yes. I'm looking forward to it. I've not seen too much of the countryside round here." she said.

"Me, neither. That story about the manager intrigued me. I wonder what his name was? I'm interested in him and want to see where he started his last journey. Abdul's quite a character."

"Yes. he's very interesting," She said.

Abdul and Jeanine were just coming out of their house, followed by Francoise and Dan Spring. Jeanine and Dan got in the front cab of the Landrover, and Francoise climbed in the open canvas covered back. Abdul climbed onto his Suzuki motorcycle. Howard walked over to talk to him.

"Do you ride?" Abdul asked.

"Yes. I was very keen when I was younger. I used to rebuild old motorcycles as a hobby. I still have an old Norton in my garage in Banbury."

"We'll swap over about halfway along then."

The convoy started off down the road past the Rest House towards the plant. Just after the plant Abdul left the main road and took a track that went down a steep hill into a valley. The weather was dry and coolish compared to the fierce heat normal for this time of the year.

The road was very bad. At one time, it had obviously been the main road but the weather and lack of maintenance had turned it into a motorist's nightmare. It was deeply rutted, with large lose rocks in places and the gradient was bad. The centre of the road was high, with grass clumps obscuring the road direction. In places, the short hills were very steep.

Abdul stopped at the first bridge they had to cross because it looked very dangerous. It was feet long and appeared to be about five feet wide. Abdul got off the motorcycle and walked across. "It's not as bad as it looks,." he said to Jeanine and Howard.

"It's worse," Howard whispered to Angeline.

Abdul appeared satisfied it would take the weight of the Landrovers, so he pushed the motorcycle across the wooden planks. Jeanine stopped and stepped onto the bridge. Howard and Angeline joined her. The bridge was ten feet above the water. Originally, it had been well built, the main support consisting of an old truck chassis. Now, the notched supporting trees looked as though they were rotting and some of the decking had been replaced with small tree branches. Howard looked down into the shallow, rocky river underneath. He hoped it didn't contain crocodiles.

"Would you like me to go first?" Howard asked Jeanine.

"No. It should be safe."

They all crossed slowly, though safely.

"Would you like to ride the motorcycle?" Abdul asked Howard.

"Yes. This reminds me of motocross riding."

Howard got on the motorcycle and Abdul got into the Landrover with Angeline Taylor.

Howard enjoyed riding the motorcyle, but couldn't see too much because the road had sunk below the level of the surrrounding countryside. What they did see had been torn up by mining machines. Only small bushes and ground vegetation remained. The area looked like a disused battlefield.

They crossed another bridge which looked sturdier.

"This small stream marks the company boundary here. The bridge is a sort of goodwill present to the local people," Mohamed said.

Howard realized this was the bridge Sean had talked about the other day.

Four hours into the journey, they came to a large river forty feet across. The old mining bridge had collapsed and had been replaced by a rickety structure of poles, planks and tree branches. Howard and Abdul changed places and Abdul rode the motorcycle across the bridge, waiting on the other side. The others got out of their vehicles and had a short conference. They decided not to drive across the bridge. Luckily two women stopped and talked to Abdul on the other side. They hitched up their long skirts and waded across the river. Jeanine drove into the river. The water level was low, so they were able to drive through. On the other side, there were cultivated rice fields and small villages. Abdul was surprised they hadn't gone across the bridge.

At last, they came to the pumping station that had been built in the French colonial days. There was a large onion-shaped water tank, a pump and generator housed in a concrete building and a house for the operator. The station supplied water and electricity to the village. Even though it was not quite dark, the generator was working for their visit. The area had been cleared of vegetation and a table set up under a thatched shelter. Nearby, the villagers had a barbeque stove made of an old oil drum from the old plant.

A small delegation consisting of five men, including the mayor of the village, was there to welcome them. After shaking hands with everyone in the Banam party, they helped put up the tents and unload the Landrovers.

Francoise started to cook steaks, chicken and sausages on the barbeque. They had brought a salad from Banam and the villagers provided rice and green vegetables for the meal.

"Cook enough," Jeanine said, "we'll invite these villagers."

The villagers provided mangoes, grapefruit and oranges, and the party was entertained by a group from the village. Howard was impressed by how much talent their was in such a small area. There was a flame thrower, magicians and musicians. The evening finished up with an impromptu French style dance, the music being provided by Jeanine on a guitar. She also sang some French songs.

Francoise left with the group and went to sleep in the village.

Howard had to use the toilet, a primitive concrete slab with a centre hole in a thatched building. Someone had provided toilet paper.

He washed in a trough used by the village women to do their laundry. It had faucets and the water was warm from the sun. He slept well on a canvas bed in a tent shared by Dan Spring. Dan had brought a bottle of brandy with him and they each had a tot before they went to sleep.

Howard was up early the next morning at first light. He liked sleeping out in a tent. It reminded him of holidays with friends on the Welsh beaches. Francoise was already up, bus cooking breakfast. She was cooking eggs, bacon, sausages and mushrooms. He knew with the nearby village, none of it would go to waste. After washing and shaving, Howard sat on a canvas chair near the table. Francoise brought him a large breakfast. After everyone had eaten, they packed up two of the tents. The other was left in place, protecting articles inside in case it rained.

Howard, Abdul, Dan, Angeline and Jeanine wanted to go and see the old plant. Francoise wanted to visit her friends in the village. While Howard and the rest drove the two Landrovers out to the old plant site, Abdul rode his motorcycle there and Francoise walked to the village. It was six miles to the old plant. As they were going along the old road, they saw it in the distance. The steel girders were still there, like giant cobwebs on some isolated planet. When they arrived, they saw it was surrounded by a graveyard of old, decrepid machinery. The steel scrap had originally come from the Soviet Union, though there were a lot of electric motors and pumps that still bore their original English markings.

The old office was still standing at the bottom of the hill. But now, part of it was a store that they saw through the main doorway. It contained agricultural hand tools, second-hand clothes, films, Russian watches and Hong Kong cameras. Rather incrongruously, a new Mercedes-Benz housed under a thatched shelter was parked by the side of the building. A uniformed chauffeur was polishing it.

As they parked the Landrovers Abdul suggested, "It's the type of place where the illicit miners buy their tools and supplies, and sell their diamonds."

As they switched off their engines, Abdul Kourouma, the old clerk, came out of a small office at the end of the building. He was a tall, slim man who, because of his colouring and figure, looked more Arabic than African. Howard estimated he must be at least sixty years old. He saw them looking at the Mercedes.

"I own a small house in England. The rent from it bought the car," He carried on. "You must be the people from the new mine at Banam? I'm Abdul Kourouma. I worked here when it was owned by a British company before the war. My house is where the manager used to live. But, I've enlarged and modernized it. We'll have lunch there."

"As long as we can have it at twelve o' clock," Colonel Abdul said.

"Yes. We can have it early if you have to get back."

Abdul showed them around the site and explained how the plant had ceased to operate after the Russians left. However, he didn't show them around his store.

At eleven o' clock, they walked up to Abdul's house. It was a large airy building, raised off the ground. It had a steep, corrugated iron roof. The central section consisted of an island of single rooms across with doors on both sides, surrounded by large verandahs fenced in with square, steel mesh wire.

Abdul gestured for them to sit in some comfortable armchairs.

"Would you like a beer?" he asked.

"Yes, please,." everybody replied.

He went away and a uniformed Guinean brought five beers in frosted glasses.

"Your English is very good, Mr. Kourouma!" Howard said.

"Yes. That was why I was hired in 1939 because I knew English," Abdul said. "Mr. Adams signed me on. He was a kind man. I've got his old motorcycle in a shed in the garden. The police brought it back here after he died. It belongs to me now."

"Can we see it?" Jeanine said.

"I don't see why not. Would you like to come, Colonel?"

"Yes."

The Banam party and Abdul walked around the back of the house to a small shed. It was dank inside, with the smell of rotting leather, rusty steel and old burned oil. But, there was a gem inside. It was a large, dirty, rusty motorcycle. Howard had heard of these marvels, but never saw one. He knew it was a Brough Superior. Even in old age, it had the look of a thoroughbred with the twin, fish-tailed exhaust pipes, black enamel and chrome.

"How marvellous," he said.

"It's not been used for over twenty years," Abdul said, "and it's over forty years old."

"I'll buy it from you.—If you want to sell it?" Howard said.

"I wouldn't sell it," Abdul said. "But I will give it to you, if you take it away from here." "We'll take it today. If I take off the front wheel, it will go in the Landrover easily."

"I'll get one of my men to do it and load it into your Landrover. If we take off the canvas cover, it will be easy. May I have your car keys?"

Howard gave them to him.

"Thanks. It is very generous of you to give it to me. I'll pay you something, if you like."

"No. I can tell you're an enthusiast and will restore it. I think it's a good thing if I get rid of it because it reminds, after all these years, of Mr. Adams death."

Howard noticed Abdul hadn't used the word 'murder' so far. Perhaps the fact that Rory Adams had been killed still upset him?

"One thing that was never recovered after Mr. Adams death was his silver whiskey flask. I always thought he took it with him on his last journey."

"What did it look like?" Howard asked.

"Well. It held about a pint and had the initials 'RHA' engraved on the side. There was a hallmark on the bottom and a dent from when Mr. Adams dropped it."

Howard's ears pricked up. He knew where the flask was now.

When they returned to the verandah, Abdul invited the party to lunch in the dining room.

After an excellent lunch, they went back to the verandah to drink coffee.

"I have the biscuit tin Mr. Adams used to transport the diamonds to Sierra Leone."

He showed Abdul and Howard a tin box about 10" by 8."

"This box was why Mr. Adams was killed," he said. "It contained the diamonds. But Mr. Adams shouldn't have gone on the motorcycle. It was too well known and noisy for the trip. Someone must have known what he was carrying. But there was no need to kill him. I always thought I should have persuaded him to go with Mr. Warner in the Ford and take guards with them. But in those days, a clerk didn't make suggestions like that to a manager. A manager's orders were always obeyed."

Howard thought he detected a hint of a guilty conscience. He sounded as though he was one of the few people who knew about the diamonds.

"Who besides you would have known about the diamonds?" Howard asked.

"Well, Mr. Warner went ahead the day before as a sort of decoy. In those days, you had to cross the Kulu by means of a ford, or go across on a boat when the river was high. Mr. Adams knew the way to the ford across the Kulu, but was unsure of the route into Sierra Leone. A guide was supposed to meet him at the river, but a sudden thunderstorm with heavy rain messed the whole thing up. Mr. Adams couldn't find the guide or cross the swollen river, so he waited till the next morning. It was this man who found his body that night and came back here. The man knew he couldn't cross the river in the storm, so he'd stayed in the village. When the rain stopped, he went down the track and found Mr. Adams. He saw the thief running away. But of course, it was too late. The thief, a deserter from the French colonial army, was caught and executed by the French. They knew it was him because he was wearing Mr. Adams watch.

The guide brought the biscuit tin back here. I hid it in the slimes dam till the end of the war. After the war, Mr. Warner, who'd been in the army, came from England and took the diamonds back to London. He was very annoyed because there were no large diamonds in the shipment. He was very rude to me and kept asking questions. He seemed convinced that I had kept the larger stones. Mr. Warner disliked Guinea and was always harsh to the workers on the mine. But Mr. Adams was the only one who knew what had been sent. London knew there should have been a lot of large diamonds because the company was trying to stockpile the more profitable stones in case of any possible disruption due to the war. The large diamonds never turned up and nobody seems to know what happened to them. Obviously, they could have been sold by now. But, it is possible they could still be lying out there in the bush. If they were hidden by Mr. Adams, the vegetation would have covered them over."

"Sounds like an interesting story. You must have been scared the Germans would find the diamonds?"

"Not really. They didn't know about them. They thought they were in Sierra Leone. Anyway, they were too busy trying to get the mine working again. Mr. Warner helped DIASA get this lease after the government changed its policies."

"What happened to the motorcycle after Mr. Adams was killed?"

"The mine workers pushed it along the road from Banam to here. One of the German officers used to ride it during the war. It hasn't been used since."

"I'm afraid we must be off," Abdul said. "I have things I must do in Banam. If you would like to visit the mine, you can stay with me and Jeanine."

"I'd like to. When would be convenient?"

"In two week's time. At the weekend. Come on Friday and I'll arrange it with the manager, Angeline's husband, so you can see the mine," Abdul said.

"Yes. I'm sure Bob won't object," Angeline said.

"We'll arrange a meal at the club on the Saturday night," Jeanine said.

"Okay. We'll see you then."

"Before you go, would you like to see Mr. Adams' grave?"

"Is he buried here?" As soon as he said it, Howard knew it was a stupid question.

"Yes. I'll show you the site. It's just behind the house."

The group walked around the side of the house, up a well-worn path made of stones to a small stone marker standing in a cleared, grassy plot. The marker was made of grey granite that had been roughly sculpted to form a block, like those used to mount horses. Cut into the stone, on top, an inscription read. *Rory Adams. Died 1940 R.I.P.*

The plot was grassed over and obviously well looked after. A few lily flowers grew near the headstone.

"We pay an old lady to look after it," Abdul said.

After saying goodbye, the Banam group left and drove back to the pumping station. Howard was thrilled with his gift that had been loaded into his Landrover. It made steering the Landrover difficult with all the weight in the back, though.

They loaded up the tents and equipment and drove down to the river. Abdul was riding the motorcycle and Dan Spring was driving the other Landrover. Some of the villagers came to see them off. Howard was amazed when a few of the villagers picked up the motorcycle and carried it across the river. The Landrovers drove through the water.

At the other side, Abdul said, "See you in Banam," and rode off.

Francoise was sitting on the tents in the back of the Landrover. Angeline was in the cab of the other Landrover which was open except for its frame. The Brough Superior 100 motorcycle was lying awkwardly in the back. Howard drove slowly, beginning to question the wisdom of acquiring such a machine. *How am I going to get it back to England?*

"Wasn't it amazing how Adbul, the clerk, refused to accept money for the Brough?"

"He very likely wanted to get rid of it. He may have felt that he had to give it to a sympathetic restorer because of the manner of its owner's death."

"The Brough Superior is famous for its links to Lawrence of Arabia. He was riding one when he died. They say he tried to avoid two children on bicycles," Howard said, sounding like a guide in a museum.

"Bob was a keen motorcyclist when we first met. He was a bricklayer at the time and we didn't have much money. We could have gotten money from my mother, but Bob wouldn't accept it. He knew my mother thought he wasn't good enough for me because I'd been to University and he hadn't. That's why I was scared of what Buzzard knew. Bob's got a marvellous chance here to get into upper management and I didn't want anyone spoiling it."

Howard couldn't understand why someone like Angeline's mother could despise someone like Bob because he had been a manual worker. Though he must be well paid. He couldn't see manager of Banam was such a big deal.

"Possibly Bob could give me tips about restoring it."

"Possibly. But we didn't have anything as exotic as a Brough. We had an old BSA before we got a used car. I believe the Brough Superior had a JAP engine. Yours will be a good souvenir of Guinea. Think of the story you can tell!"

"I wonder if the manager that the clerk talked about had any relatives?"

"I should imagine so. The DIASA office in Banbury could find out."

The conversation dried up after that. Howard enjoyed his talk with Angeline and now thought she wasn't as snobbish as he had previously thought. The other Landrover, going at a faster speed, arrived back long before they did. On the way, Howard noticed an odd thing about a well-used path he saw along the stream that was also a DIASA boundary. The path was on the DIASA side of the stream. Being an ex-policeman, he wondered why. *Shouldn't it be on the other side?* He decided to bring some of his men to see what it was used for."

Howard dropped Angeline and her luggage off at her house. He then drove down to the club to see if Tom Gough was inside.

Tom came out to talk to Howard. "What the hell have you got there. It looks monstrous."

"It's a Brough Superior. It's not been used for years. I'm going to rebuild it. I think everything is here."

"What can I do for you?" Tom asked.

"I want somewhere to keep it. I thought your washsite would be ideal."

"Yes. We have plenty of room. I could put it near the bottom of the site and build a shelter over it. I've got some aluminium sheets and will get the labourers to build the shelter tomorrow. We'd better get some labourers from the village to unload it and cover it with a tarpaulin. Have you got some dollars?"

"Yes. I always have some in my wallet."

"A dollar apiece should do it."

They drove down to the washsite. Tom Gough went to the village and came back with six labourers.

They pushed the Brough off the back of the Landrover and covered it with a tarpaulin from the Washsite store. Howard handed out the dollars and the men left happy.

"One of Mr. Adams' old mechanics works in the washsite. He can help you clean up the motorcycle," one of the labourers said before he left.

"Thanks for telling me."

"Let's go and have a drink at the club. I'll make some sandwiches to go with the drinks," Tom said.

Howard drove up to his house for a quick washup and went back to the club.

He stayed there with Tom until they left at ten o' clock.

CHAPTER 16

HE NEXT MORNING after he had eaten and dressed for work he decided to speak to Tom Gough about the flask he had. He hadn't done it last night. He'd wanted to ask a favour then and wanted to keep his questioning separate from his normal life.

As he was driving to the Security Office, he saw Tom Gough leaving the Washsite in his Landrover. He waited for him outside the ofiice. Howard knew he could leave the camp area because Abdul would answer any radio messages and deal with any other business. When Tom arrived, with a couple of his men in the back of his Landrover he stopped to talk to him.

"What are you doing today, Tom?"

"Ttoday, we're taking samples at Block Six. It's two miles from the plant. We're trying to designate some high grade blocks near the plant. The plant can minc thcm easily and the company will have money to pay for the heavy capital expenditure, necessary at this stage of development. We need a lot of money to pay for buildings, infrastructure and heavy machinery. Building a mine miles from the coast doesn't come cheap.

"Do you mind if I come along to see how samples are taken?"

"No. Be my guest. It's all straightforward. The field has been marked by the Survey people from Matakourou and we just dig at the pegged locations. It's done on a grid system. Here, it's marked 200' by 100'. It's a rich area, but sometimes we do 400' by 200' to see if there's anything there. We try to establish blocks for the Mining Department. It's like one of those children's puzzles where you join all the letters together. These maps can be dangerous for DIASA because if the illegals get them they know where the diamonds are."

"But there are no illegals around here?"

"Not so far. Let's hope there're not just waiting for us to do the prospecting for them."

"You're a cynic, Tom."

"No. I've been too long in the diamond industry. It does that to you. You saw the abandoned mine at the weekend. What do you think the former employees are doing now?"

"I'll come in my Landrover for convenience," Howard said.

"Okay. Just follow me out to the site. The Poclain driver went out with the tractor and trailor to start digging."

Tom Gough drove along the road to the plant. Just before they reached the plant, they took a newly made-road. It had been freshly graded and carried on for two miles. It ended abruptly at a flat parking area that contained pumps, hoses and a trailor. The two men left their vehicles in the parking area and walked to where they saw the Poclain machine standing.

"Be careful you don't step into one of the old filled pits," Tom said. "Sometimes they're still full of water underneath. I was lucky one day because we kept hitting rock and I kept relocating the pit in a small area and forgot and stepped into one. I went down quickly and came up like a cork in a bottle. Luckily, the Poclain driver noticed me and pulled me out. when I floated to the top."

The Poclain machine was in the middle of the cleared site, standing by a partially finished hole.

"I told him to start so we could finish quickly. Today, I want to get two samples that we can wash after lunch. We have to get results every day this week, instead of every other day as normal. Normally, we dig one day and wash the next. I think the company may be having cash flow problems. The easy way out is to mine a rich block and sell the diamonds quickly. When the plant at Matakourou starts, the company will be profitable. It's a large rich area. Let's show you how we do it."

"How many years have you been working in diamond mining?"

"About 25. Though I've worked in Africa for about 35 years. I was in the navy during the war and afterwards went out to Kenya as a farm manager. After spending a lot of time at sea in small ships, I didn't want to be surrounded by a lot of people and buildings. Later on, during the Mau Mau business, I was a contract police officer."

"I'm still amazed at people working in these lonely places for so many years."

"I suppose it grows on you. The hot weather, servants, good salaries, no taxes and the parties. At one time, we were in places like Ghana, Sierra Leone or Tanzania. But now, a lot of countries have nationalized the mining companies and employ their own people. This will be my last tour because I don't think the company will renew my contract. It depends on my medical exam before I go on leave. Last time, the doctor told me my weight and blood pressure were too high and I must cut down on the booze. As you know, I haven't. I had to see a London specialist last time and I don't think he will let me come back this time. I'm over sixty, so I' m ready to retire. The only problem is that I don't have a pension and haven't saved up much money because of the drinking. Though, I think I'm still young enough to get some kind of a job in England. After sixty five I can collect my pension."

"I don't think I will do more than two six-month tours here. Though I'd like to show Jean this place. Otherwise, she might never believe it."

"Feel like a drink before we start?" Tom said.

"No. It's much too early."

"Suit yourself. I'm going to have one."

Tom produced a silver flask and took a long gulp. Before he could put it back in his bag, Howard asked, "That's an unusual flask. Where'd you get it?"

"I bought it from Mark Buzzard one evening. We were drinking at his house one night and I admired the flask. 'You can have it', he said. I protested it was too valuable to give away but he told me he had given ten pounds to one of his security men for it. So, I gave him ten pounds and he seemed happy enough to give it to me."

"Can I see it?"

"Yes. Why not?"

Tom handed over the half-empty flask. It was the one Abdul, the clerk, had described. The initials RHA were engraved on the side. There was a small dent and a Dublin hallmark underneath. Howard knew it was the Dublin hallmark because it had a harp stamped on it.

"You wouldn't like to sell it to me at a large profit, I suppose?"

"No. It's a souvenir of this place now. Of Mark and Guinea. I would only drink the money anyway. At least I have this."

"Would you mind if I take a photograph of it when we get back to camp? I have a Polaroid camera."

"No. Not at all. But why are you interested in it?"

"Well, I've got the Brough Superior as a souvenir and the flask would complement it. I think it belonged to the Brough's owner. But a photo will do."

"Sorry to disappoint you. But let's start working."

Howard realized Tom didn't want to talk about the flask.

Tom dropped his weighted tape measure down the hole to measure the distance to the bottom. He then wrote it in his notebook with a description of the soil type—in this case, clay. Tom waved to the Poclain operator to carry on digging. The operator operated various hydraulic levers to open the clamshell attachment, bored into the bottom of the hole, closed the clamshell and then raised it to the surface. Tom looked at the material in the clamshell and motioned the operator to discard it by the side of the pit. This measuring, digging and discarding continued until Tom saw gravel in the clamshell. This material was discarded in the trailer. When the machine reached the bedrock below the gravel, the excavation was stopped. Tom wrote a sample ticket for the trailer and the tractor drove away to the parking area, coming back with the other one. The Poclain refilled the hole with the discarded material from the side of the pit.

"These are easy pits because they're what we call terrace pits. You don't get much water and the sides are stable. If they're nearer the river it's much more difficult because water comes in and we have to use a casing shield. We move it with the machine and attach chains to position it and remove it. The sample is taken from inside the casing. But these pits are all terrace pits."

When the tractor and trailor returned, they finished the second pit.

"I'll start washing the first sample—which is the second by the way—when the tractor arrives at the Washsite," Tom said. "They want quick results for Banbury."

"I won't bother to see you wash the sample but I would like to get the photograph today."

"Well, take the flask and return it to me in the Washsite."

Tom handed the flask to Howard who walked back to his Landrover. He drove to the plant to see if everything was alright there. It was, so he drove back to Banam.

On the way, he thought about the flask and how it was connected with Buzzard's death. He resolved to question his security men and find out if anyone of them had sold the flask to Mark Buzzard. First, he decided to tell Abdul of his findings.

Abdul was sitting in his office when Howard walked in.

"Things are moving," he said. "The examining magistrate, Ibrahim Diallo, is coming here next Monday to question Tamba and anyone else he feels like."

"That's good because I've found out something interesting." Like a magician, Howard produced the silver flask he had obtained from Tom Gough.

"Voila," he said. "Regardez Bien."

"What the hell's that?" Abdul asked.

"This is possibly the flask that Rory Adams was carrying when he was killed forty odd years ago."

"This business gets stranger and stranger. Where did you get it?"

"From Tom Gough, the Prospecting Superviser. He says he bought it from Buzzard. Buzzard supposedly bought it from one of the security men. I'm going to ask them now if they know anything about it."

Abdul took the flask from Howard and examined it.

"The initials presumably stood for Rory Adams. The hallmark underneath should give us a date and a year? But remember the knife you found with the initials RHA? I wonder if it belonged to Rory?"

"Yes I think so. But coming back to the flask.—I have a book of hallmarks in my house and will look it up. I'm sure the harp must signify it was made in Dublin. We can check with Abdul, the clerk, when he comes next week to see if this is the flask."

"I'll question the security men if you like?" Abdul said. "It might be easier."

"Yes. That would be a great help. I'll just go and photograph the flask because Tom doesn't want to sell it and I think we should have something on record of its existence. It may mean Tom has something to do with Buzzard's death."

"Don't jump to conclusions. I'll question the men and let you know in the morning if I find out anything."

"Okay. I'm going out to the plant after lunch and then back to the Washsite."

Howard did what he said and spent a boring afternoon at the Washsite with Tom Gough. They did not discuss the silver flask.

Howard spent the evening in his house. For some reason, he felt very homesick. He remembered a similar feeling when he left Wales. Now the feeling was stronger. He wasn't married to Jean and part of her family, back then. He wondered how he had been so stupid as to risk his happiness with Jean for the sake of a dubious business partnership with a friend. *I must have been insane,* he thought. What surprised him was his feelings for Wales had changed. He knew now that when Jean delivered their child, his love for her would be at least as strong as his love for Wales.

He still had the Banbury Guardian newspaper he had bought the Thursday before he left England and read it from the front page to the back. He loved reading the titbits from the village correspondents. The villages and towns had marvellous English names; the Bourtons, Bloxam, Chipping Norton, Chipping Warden, Wardington, and the rest. He had read somewhere that Chipping signified a market town and Warden meant a badger's den.

It was still light around six o' clock, so he decided to take a walk to try to shake off his homesickness. By the time he came from his walk up and down the hill he realized his homesickness was normal for someone in his circumstances. He went into the club and had a beer with Bob Taylor.

He went home and cooked himself a meal of curry and rice before relaxing again. He read a mystery novel he had brought with him and wrote a letter to Jean. He told her all about the old mine, their trip there and how he'd met the old clerk. He also told her how the clerk had given him the old Brough Superior motorcycle belonging, to Rory Adams. He asked her if she could get an old manual for a Brough Superior 100 motorcycle. She could try the bookshops, like W.H. Smith, or ask one of his old police friends to help find a specialist bookshop. He stressed she should only send it out to Banam by someone who was coming out to the mine. He finished the letter by telling her how much he loved her and how he missed her.

The next morning, he asked Abdul, "Did you find out anything about the flask?"

"No. Everyone denies any knowledge of it. That doesn't mean too much because they may not want to get involved in a police inquiry."

CHAPTER 17

O N WEDNESDAY, HOWARD received a Banbury Guardian newspaper and two letters from Jean. He had warned her in one of his early letters not to send any parcels through the postal system, as they frequently got lost. He was expecting her to send him a video tape of her life and family's doings. But, he would have to wait until someone arrived from England.

On Thursday evening, when he was drinking in the bar Bob Taylor mentioned the trip he wanted to do on Sunday. "I'm organizing a trip to the Table Top Hill on Sunday. The locals call it the Devil's mountain. Would you like to come? So far, Angeline and I are going with the Kouroumas and Dan Spring. Jeffrey Ellis will come and organize the food. Tom Gough will look after the bar in his absence. Henry Hardcastle and Tom never seem to go anywhere. Henry only seems to work and stay in his house. He doesn't even drink much. I asked him if he'd like to go, and he said 'no'. I believe he likes to read alot."

"Yes, I'd like to see a bit more of the countryside and I enjoyed the trip to the old mine. That flat-topped hill looks interesting," Howard said.

"Okay. We'll take cold boxes for the food and drinks. We can take soft drinks and beer with salads, water for coffee, charcoal and a grill for the barbeque. There must be stones on the slopes of the hill for a barbeque pit. Francoise and her brother, Mohamed, would love to come and they can help with the food. They like that kind of thing anyway, and I'll give them food and money as a bonus."

"What time shall we set off?"

"If we start at nine o' clock, it will be cooler. Apparently, there's an easy path up the hill and a flat place about halfway. We'll put the barbeque there. Without shade on top, it will be stinking hot. We'll take large golfing umbrellas for shade and canvas chairs to sit on," Bob said. "But don't worry about food because Jeffrey will make it in the club. We'll have the normal meal at the club on Saturday night, and leave food for the stay behinds. We'll go in three Landrovers and Abdul will go on his motorcycle. Jeanine can go with you in your Landrover."

Before nine o' clock on Sunday morning, Howard and Jeanine set out in Howard's loaded Landrover for the trip to the flat topped hill. This hill had intrigued Howard ever since he had been in Banam. It was so unusual, sticking out of a flat countryside like a sandcastle on a sandy beach, as though it was guarding the Banam valley. It reminded Howard of the Wrekin in Shropshire, England. He was looking forward to the climb to the top and the subsequent view.

Francoise was in the back of the Landrover that had the canopy open at the rear. Howard thought she looked attractive in the light blue dress that Jeanine had given her. Jeanine looked very cool and attractive in a pair of yellow shorts and a pink shirt.

The trip to the base of the hill took two hours. The road had been graded and was in good condition. Because it was a hot, dry day, Howard's main problem was the dust stirred up by the motorcycle out in front. He found it very difficult to breathe and kept slowing down to allow the clouds of dust to settle. The heat shimmering off the baked road made it difficult to see too far ahead, as well.

Howard and Jeanine talked about the trip to the old mine and the upcoming visit of the examining judge, Ibrahim Diallo.

"His wife, Fiona, is Scottish. It's a romantic story. They met in France at the beginning of World War Two. He was a sergeant, attached to a French battalion, and she was a nurse at a British Military Hospital. They both went to England from Dunkirk when they evacuated the troops. They were married in England. After the war, he studied law in Paris, but returned here when Guinea became independent. He's stayed away from political controversy as much as possible and has an awesome reputation as a judge."

"Are they going to stay at your house?"

"No, they'll stay at the Rest House. I don't think they'll stay at Banam for more then one night. The judge can question people in Matakourou, or even Kissidougou if he wants. He's very likely come here to give a party and meet people. Abdul will do a lot of the work. There's no hurry till we have the result of the inquest from England. They might say it was an accident."

By now, they had arrived at the base of the hill and pulled into an area that Abdul had cleared with his cutless. He was engaged in enlarging the area by hacking away at the vegetation.

""Just park anywhere," he said.

Howard pulled into a space and he, Jeanine and Francoise unloaded the Landrover.

Howard found himself a shady spot under a small shrub, unfolded one of the chairs, took a cold beer from one of the cold boxes and sat down. Jeanine went over to talk to Abdul. They both came back and sat down near Howard.

"Have a rest Francoise until the others arrive. Get yourself a soft drink," Jeanine said.

"Thank you, Madame," Francoise said, rather formally.

Within a few minutes, the other two Landrovers arrived in clouds of dust. They were soon unloaded with everyone working together.

"It looks more like an expedition to Mount Everest than a hike up a small hill," Dan Spring said, sarcastically.

"There's no need to rough it, even in the bush, if you don't need to," Jeffrey Ellis said in reply. "Remember, we were up early this morning getting the food ready."

"I didn't mean to be rude," Dan said, apologetically.

"Let's get the food and things from base camp to camp two," Bob Taylor said, trying to be jovial. "Remember, I don't want anyone who's driving to get so drunk they can't drive safely.".

"I'm riding the motorcycle, so I'll be a good Muslim today," Abdul said.

"I'll drive if you don't mind, Howard?" Jeanine said. "But I will have a glass of wine."

"I'm not a good drinker, so I'll drive," Angeline said. "That means you can drink, Bob."

"Thanks."

Jeffrey Ellis and Mohamed carried up a portable barbeque and a sack of charcoal to the flat area half-way up the hill. This area was shaded by the shrubs above. The path carried on up the hill to the large flat area on top.

"I hope someone brought a ball?" Dan Spring asked.

"I organized it," Jeffrey said, "Of course I brought a ball. A large rubber one. I didn't think we could manage a leather one."

Mohamed and Francoise set up the barbeque and got the charcoal burning. The rest of the group walked up to the top of the hill. Dan Spring carried the basketball.

The large flat area on the top was the size of a small soccer field.

"Don't get too enthusiatic and fall off the edge." Howard said.

After Abdul, Dan, Bob and Howard kicked the ball backwards and forwards for about ten minutes, they gave up. It was much too hot on the exposed flat hill and it was definitely too dangerous.

"We'll play at the bottom after lunch," Bob Taylor said. "Let's just admire the view."

"It is spectacular!" Angeline Taylor said. "Isn't that Matatkourou the other side of the river over there?"

"Yes, that's it. You can see the radio masts," Bob said.

The group stayed on top of the hill for another half hour and then decided to go down for lunch.

Lunch was ready when they arrived at the grille, and it was a very slow, torpid event. The weather had changed very quickly. A cool, cloudy day suddenly became a superheated cloudless one. The group visibly wilted. It was though the hot sun had sucked every bit of energy out of them. By three o' clock, everyone was ready to go back to the camp and get out of the heat. The ride back was torturous. The dust from the road seemed to find every gap in Howard's clothing. It intruded and stuck to his sweating body. He could see Jeanine was just as uncomfortable. On the ride back to Banam, she reminded Howard about the judges's visit the next day.

When the Landrovers and Abdul's motorcycle arrived back at the camp, everyone quickly helped unload the vehicles and went back to their houses. It was too hot to do anything but lie down until the heat subsided. Howard had not realized how hot it could get in Guinea till today. When he went inside his house, he was soaked in sweat. Except for his shorts, he took off all his clothes, opened all the windows and switched on the fan he had bought in Matakourou. The air, ciculating around the blades of the fan, wafted over his body. A half an hour later, he felt cooler. He heaved himself off his bed, staggered to the refrigorater, took out two bottles of beer and drank them. He then put on a pair of trainers and walked up to the top of the hill above the cabins. When he reached the top, there was a breeze blowing. He felt cooler. He walked down the hill after a few minutes and went into the bar.

Only Tom Gough was there. It was obvious he was drunk. Howard didn't want to go back to his empty cabin, so helped himself to a beer from the fridg and talked to Tom. After two beers, however, he went back to his lonely house, stripped off his clothes, and went to sleep.

CHAPTER 18

O N MONDAY MORNING Howard awoke with a throbbing headache. It was early, six am and already light and he was needed to get dressed. The searing heat of the previous afternoon had been replaced by a cool, morning breeze. He leapt out of bed, stretched and went into the bathroom. It was so good to be alive. After a quick, cool shower, he was ready to confront the day.

He abruptly realised that today was the day the judge and his wife were coming. He shaved very carefully and put on his best starched, khaki uniform and creased slacks. After breakfast, he decided to talk to Bob Taylor. He walked down to the offices where Bob was already at work.

"Morning, Howard. You already for the visit?"

"As ready as ever. We might get some answers today. I'm intrigued by the way Buzzard's death is linked with the loss of a diamond shipment forty years prior. I believe the French system with examining judges can be very effective."

"I wanted to talk to you about your role in the proceedings. I think it best if you let Abdul do most of the questioning with the judge. The company doesn't want to appear to be running the investigation. Obviously, we're concerned about Buzzard's death, but we don't wish to jeopardize our investment here."

"But if Abdul asks me to be present. That's Okay, isn't it?"

"Yes, of course. But don't be too aggressive. The women will entertain Fiona, the judge's wife. Jeanine knows her. They're arriving in an army helicopter about nine. They'll only spend the ne night here. I think the judge wants to see where Mark died."

"Is Tamba Suluku going to be here?"

"Yes. He's been in jail in Kissidougou. Aafterwards, he'll go back there."

"What do you want me to do now?" Howard asked.

"Just stick around until the judge arrives."

"Can I go and have a talk with Abdul?"

"Okay,. as long as I know where you are," Bob said.

Howard walked along to the security offices and went into Abdul's. He was sitting at his desk, talking to a man in police uniform.

"Morning, Abdul."

"Morning, Howard. This is Sekou Troare, the judge's secretary and shorthand expert. The helicopter should arrive about 8.30. I'd like you to be present when the judge questions Seluku."

"Thanks. I'd like to be there."

Howard walked into his own office. He checked with the radio operator. There weren't any messages.

At eight o' clock, he heard the sound of a very noisy helicopter coming from the direction of Matakourou. It landed in the compound in a cloud of dust and debris. The engine was switched off and the rotors slowly stopped turning. A forward door opened, the pilot stepped out of the craft and walked around to the other side. He opened the rear door and a tall, grey-haired, distinguished looking Guinean dressed in a khaki uniform stepped out. He was followed by a slight, elegant, grey-haired English woman. She was dressed in a long, light pink coloured, chintz fabric dress. Howard thought she looked overdressed for this basic type of camp.

As they walked from the helicopter, Howard, Abdul, Bob Taylor, Angeline and Jeanine approached to greet the visitors.

"Bonjour, Henri. Bonjour, Fiona. Sa va bien?" Jeanine asked.

"Fine and yourself?" Fiona replied in English.

"We're Okay."

The judge and his wife were introduced to everyone.

"Fiona, If you come with us we'll go to Angeline's house. You ready for the official visit, Angeline?"

"Yes. You'll just have to take what we've got. This isn't Paris or Conakry, you know?"

"I'm sure everything will be first rate," Fiona said in a conciliatory manner.

The women walked away to Angeline's house.

"Come to Angeline's for lunch," Jeanine called to Abdul.

"Will do."

The judge seemed eager to start his inquiry.

"Where can we question Tamba Suluku?"

"I suggest we use the Security Office," Abdul said.

"That will do fine."

"I'll see you at lunch time," Bob Taylor said. "But I shall be in my office, if you need me."

Howard's office had been transformed, while he was away. A table had been added to the desk to make a larger writing surface. The interpreter was sitting in front of the desk with a large chair for the judge. There were chairs for Abdul and Howard behind the table. Tamba Suluku as sitting on a chair in front of the table, an armed guard by his side.

"Can we get some coffee, Adbul?"

"Yes, I'll send one of my men to the club."

Abdul went outside and arranged for the coffee."

"How do you like Guinea?" the judge asked Howard. "I'm interested in you opinion. You don't have to be diplomatic with me."

"I find the people very friendly."

"That's because they think you can help them attain a better life. From what I've heard, you treat them reasonably. Guineans appreciate fair people."

Howard was a bit surprised by the judge's remark. He realized he had never considered his men's reaction to himself.

"Thank you."

When the coffee came, they drank some and started their work.

When they were all seated, the judge looked at Tamba Suluku and spoke to him in his local language. He then translated into English for Howard's benefit.

"You know, Tamba, this is a serious business. Let's have the complete truth without any lies. How did you get involved with Mr. Buzzard?"

Like most Africans, Tamba Suluku was a good speaker and didn't seem to be intimidated by the judge's presence. He told his story in a direct, unhurried manner. This time, Abdul Kourouma did the translating.

"About two weeks before his death, Mr. Buzzard talked to me when we were at one of the mining blocks. We arranged to meet in the evening near the river. There, Mr. Buzzard said he had heard I could sell some diamonds for him."

"He didn't say who'd told him that?" the judge asked.

"No, But it must have been someone in England because none of the expatriates here sells through me."

"Yes. The illegal diamond trade is worldwide. They have agents everywhere," the judge said. "But he could have heard you were a dealer from one of his men, couln't he?"

"Yes. That's possible. I just wanted to sell his diamonds."

"He never said how many he had.?" the judge asked.

"He wanted me to sell three diamonds for him. I said I'd let him know and sent a note to Abdul, the old plant clerk. Leila went with her cousin on his motorcycle. Abdul told me when to deliver the diamonds and for me to ask Mr. Buzzard how he wanted to be paid. Abdul pays in gold coins or credits a bank account in Paris. I delivered the diamonds to Abdul and carried on to Kissidougou, as though going shopping. Abdul gave me a tape recorder on the way back."

"So, everthing went well?"

"Yes. There were no problems till I came back. I came back before it got dark and stayed at the plant, drinking till eleven o' clock. When I got to the village, Leila wasn't there so I went to look for her on my motorcycle. That's when I saw Mr. Evans and Leila on the path from the river."

"So, you're saying you never saw Mr. Buzzard alive that evening?"

"That's true. So help me God, I didn't kill him."

"He never said anything about any other diamonds?" the judge asked.

"No."

"Let's have another short break for coffee?" the judge said. "Abdul, can you send for Tamba's wife?"

"Yes, Sir." Abdul sent one of his security men to find Leila.

"Tamba, I'm not going to detain you. Go to your house for the time being until we decide what to do with you."

"Thank you, Sir."

Tamba walked out to his house, relieved that he hadn't been detained.

"Howard . . . you don't mind me calling you Howard, do you?" the judge asked.

"No, of course not."

"Let's talk outside. You stay here, Abdul."

The judge and Howard walked outside, far enough away so the people inside couldn't hear what they were saying.

"Howard, you're new to Guinea so I'd like to explain a few things. The government is keen to find out what happened to Mr. Buzzard. Some of the other things, however, like Tamba selling diamonds, we're not too keen on publicizing. I don't think he murdered Mr. Buzzard. So, after a time, he'll just carry on working for DIASA like before. So far, we've no concrete evidence that Mr. Buzzard had found a cache of diamonds."

"That's true enough. But what about the clerk at the old mine? He should be questioned."

"He will be. I've already sent someone to see him. What I'm trying to emphasize is that we should concentrate on Buzzard's death—not the diamonds."

"I understand you, Sir."

When they returned inside, Leila was waiting to be questioned. She was not as composed as her husband and looked nervously at the judge.

"Just tell the truth and you won't get into trouble," the judge said when he sat down.

"Now, you said you went home after the fight with Mr. Buzzard. Is that absolutely true?"

"Not exactly." Leila was twisting her hands, nervously.

"Well, what happened?" The judge spoke more harshly, as though sensing she was holding something back.

"I went to Mr. Gough's house because I was upset and frightened of what Mr. Buzzard might do. I clean his house and do his laundry, and he's always been nice to me. But, he'd been drinking and was tired. So, after two beers, I had a shower and we went to bed. I woke up later on and decided to see if Mr. Buzzard had gotten home safely. That's when I found him."

"Okay, Leila. You can go now. But stay near the village, so we can find you again if we have more questions," the judge said. "I suppose we'd better talk to Mr. Gough," he said to Howard.

"I'll go and get him," Howard said.

"Yes. If you will, please," the judge replied.

Howard walked up the hill to the Prospecting Washsite and went into the Sorting Office. "Can you close down for about an hour, Tom? The judge from Conakry wants to talk to you about Buzzard's death."

"Okay. Though I don't know how I can help?"

"Well, just tell your story and stick to the truth. The judge seems to know what he's doing."

Howard waited while Tom locked his diamonds in the safe and locked the doors around the office. They walked across the compound down the hill to the Security Office.

The judge seemed impatient to finish his inquiry and started as soon as Tom and Howard sat down. "Mr. Gough. Did Leila, Tamba's wife, come to your house the night Mr. Buzzard died?"

Howard admired the judge's direct approach.

"Yes," Tom said. "She said she had a fight with Mark and wanted to tell someone about it. She chose me because she does my cleaning and I talk to her. She knew I was a friend of Mark Buzzard."

"So, she only came to see you because she wanted to talk to someone? There was no sex involved?"

"No, I was too drunk anyway. After we talked, I fell asleep. When I woke up, she had gone. I walked down to the washsite to see if she was there, but she wasn't. That's all I know."

"So, you didn't hear of Mr. Buzzard's death until the next morning?" the judge asked.

"That's true."

"You can go, Mr. Gough. Thanks for your help," the judge said.

Howard interupted. "Tom, don't you own a silver flask that may have originally belonged to the manager of that old plant down the valley?"

"I told you I bought it off Mark Buzzard. Matakourou market has plenty of stores selling things like that. I don't know where he got it."

"But I thought you said he bought it off one of his men?"

"No, I'm sure I said in the market."

The judge interupted.

"You can go now, Mr. Gough. We can contact you again, if necessary."

When Gough had left, the judge turned to Howard. "Howard. we don't need to worry about Tom Gough. If he killed Mr. Buzzard, it could have been an accident. He doesn't look as though he wants to run away. Let's just collect the evidence first."

"I suppose you're right, Sir. But I think it has to be him, or Tamba."

"It could have been anyone in the camp, Mr. Evans, that's the problem. What about Leila? She could have pushed Buzzard down the hole. He very likely was so drunk, he just fell in the hole. The whole episode is so indistinct. Tamba is the only one who seems to know about the diamonds. Abdul, the old clerk, will know if the flask was the manager's. I think I have enough evidence for today. I'm going for lunch and afterwards, Bob Taylor is going to take us to see the plant and mining. I'll see you tonight at the club party."

Howard realized he was being dismissed, so walked back to his house for lunch.

In the evening, there was a party at the club for the judge and his wife. Howard didn't have any conversation with them until he said goodnight.

When he arrived at the office in the morning, he only had a few words with the judge and his wife before they left in the helicopter.

With the departure of the judge, Howard discussed with Abdul a project he'd had in mind for some time.

"Abdul, I'd like to take a look at the end of the pathway running along the boundary stream on the way to the old mine. I think our new men are ready now."

"I agree. We should definitely see what's going on in some of the more neglected areas."

It was arranged that they would take five men from the camp and use the ten men stationed near the stream.

On the chosen night, the weather was good and there was a moon. Abdul had an army pistol and Howard had a pickaxe handle for protection. Howard drove his own Landrover and Abdul drove the Manager's Landrover. They also had one of the mining trucks with a driver. The men were divided among the three vehicles.

Firstly, they picked up the men from Banam and then they drove out to the temporary camp near the boundary stream for the ten new men. They parked the vehicles near the bridge and followed the path. The track was very worn, but Howard could see it had been used recently. He led the way along the track, using his flashlight to follow the track. Abdul followed the security men who were sandwiched between the two senior officers. It took an hour to where the track led. There they noticed a huge excavation fifty feet by twenty. It was ten feet deep. Soil was piled up around the top of the pit. Howard shone his flashlight into the hole. There was no one there now. He could tell by the disturbed soil and gravel at the bottom men had been working there recently.

"Bring me the buckets and ropes we've brought," he said to his sergeant. "We'll take some of the gravel back with us."

"Yes, Sir."

Two of the security men produced shovels and filled up four buckets of gravel which they carried back to Howard's Landrover.

"Let's go back to the Landrovers," Howard said toAbdul, "we're not going to catch anybody tonight."

"No. But I think we've made a good start".

The security group drove back to Banam, dropping off the bridge security men on the way. Howard decided to keep an eye on his men in the temporary camp.

He'd noticed that Abdul could keep his ideas secret until ready to reveal them. So he wasn't too surprised when Abdul suggested they go out by themselves one night. "I've been talking to some of the men who used to work at the old mine. I've found out the area where we were the other night, though we thought to be mined out, is still profitable and produces the occasional large diamond. I think at least one of our security men out there helps one of the gangs and warns them when we are in the area. I'd like to test this theory by going out there with a camera to see if we can get photographs of any illegal digging. The sooner the better. What about tonight?"

"You mean we should go out there by ourselves?"

"Yes! Why not? I think it's the only way we're going to catch anybody. With evidence I can get the government to help. This time, we'll use one of the old mining roads from the other direction. Don't tell anyone."

"Okay. I'll meet you at ten o' clock tonight outside your house." Howard was amazed how quickly Abdul could act when necessary.

At ten o'clock, Howard went to Abdul's house with his Landrover.

"You'd better drive," Howard said, "you know where we're going."

So Abdul drove out of the camp, along the road to the old mine. This time, they branched off and took a smaller road. Howard was interested to see the road was obviously still being used by vehicles.

"I think we're onto something tonight. This road is obviously being used. Possibly by the IDM?" Abdul said.

Abdul stopped the Landrover and drove off into an old quarry that had once been used for repairing the roads. The original cleared surface was now covered with large bushes. Abdul hid the Landrover behind one of them. The weather was dry and cool a few insects buzzing around and occasionally zooming in to bite one of them.

The two men, carrying flashlights, cameras, Abdul's revolver and the pickaxe handle, walked along a track that led into the large excavation they had discovered the other night. Tonight was different. Approaching from the opposite direction, they heard sounds coming from the pit. They crept forward, cautiously, and peered into the pit. It was full of people. Both Abdul and Howard pointed their cameras at the mass of people and took three photographs each. They only took three because when the flashes went off, the diggers in the pit all started running in different directions.

"Don't try to catch anyone!" Abdul cautioned. "It's too dangerous for just the two of us. We have the photos. I just want proof to show to the police. "

"Okay. That makes sense. Though it would be useful to take a couple of prisoners."

"We're a long way from the camp and I don't want to get into a situation where I might have to use my revolver."

The walk back to the Landrover and subsequent drive back to Banam was uneventful.

The next day when Howard and Abdul developed their film from the diggings, they discovered that one of the photographs showed one of the diggers to be one of the security men from the temporary camp.

"I think we'd better question him to see how many of the others are involved," Abdul said.

"Yes. I don't think we've started out too well with recruiting honest security personnel," Howard replied.

"Don't be too hard on yourself. We're bound to get a few bad eggs."

Howard discovered only four of his ten guards were not involved in the illegal diggings.

CHAPTER 19

URING OCTOBER, HOWARD had a quiet time. Though, he did have an interesting experience when he went fishing with Abdul. He was surprised to find that Abdul had two fishing rods, lines and reels.

"I learned to fish by going out with my father. He learned it from the French when Guinea was a French colony. The French loved to fish. You can catch large fish like tilapia and nile perch in the Kulu." Abdul said.

"I'd like to go sometime," Howard said.

One Saturday after lunch, they collected the rubber boat from its box and set out in Howard's Landrover.

"We have to use the boat because the best place I know is some distance away from the road. It's easy to reach by boat," Abdul explained.

They drove out to the plant and stopped on top of a small hill.

"We'll leave the Landrover here and carry the boat down to the river. The Landrover will be quite safe," Abdul said.

The hill was covered with clumps of withered, straw-like grass. The red soil between the grass clumps was criss-crossed with runnels.

"Years ago, the local people used to graze their cattle here. The government stopped them because there were too many cattle and it was destroying the vegetation and polluting the river. I like it because no one seems to come here now," Abdul said.

They carried the deflated boat a quarter of a mile to the river. Abdul had brought a foot pump, so they filled it with air, put it in the river and paddled off, down stream.

Fifteen minutes later, they pulled into the river bank, hauled out the boat and fishing gear jumped out. Howard could tell this area wasn't used. The grass near the river was greener and thicker.

It was very pleasant, standing on the bank and watching the float bobbing along the river. Howard did not catch anything. Abdul, who was obviously an experienced fisherman, caught a tilapia.

"I'll get Jeanine to cook it for supper tonight. Let's hurry back before it gets dark."

The two men dismantled the rods and put them in their bags. The trip on the river was more strenuous, as they were paddling against the river current. Without any warning, it started to rain. When they arrived where they had left their Landrover. They deflated the boat and Howard carried it up the hill. The runnels in the hill started to fill with water. Halfway up, Abdul stopped and pointed to a small puddle. "What's that?" he asked. "There's something shining on the bottom."

Howard wanted to get out of the rain. "It can't be anything important."

"It think it's a largish diamond."

"Surely you don't find diamonds on a hill like this."

"You do. Some of the larger diamonds are only a half metre down."

Abdul bent down and picked up what, to Howard, looked like a piece of discoloured, glass.

"Are you sure it's a diamond?" Howard asked.

"I think so. We'd better take it back with us."

When they arrived back at the camp, Abdul and Howard took the diamond to show to Bob Taylor who confirmed it was a diamond. "I'll lock it in the safe until Monday and then take it out to the plant. Howard, on Monday, I'd like you to show me where you found the diamond."

"It was Abdul who actually found it. I didn't even know you could discover diamonds on a hillside."

"Well, many thanks, Abdul."

"It's just part of my job."

Later, on Howard partook of a very well-cooked tilapia supper prepared by Jeanine.

Some weeks later however, Abdul wasn't too pleased when his favourite fishing spot became a mining block. His quiet hillside was stripped of vegetation and machines ripped it apart to remove the gravel The river was diverted so the river bed gravel could be taken to the plant.

It was during this time he did a lot of work on the Brough Superior whenever he had any spare time. Looking through the tool box, he discovered an old, corroded, discoloured tobacco tin. It contained rusty nuts, bolts and washers of different sizes. When he emptied it out he was surprised to discover an old, silver-plated cigarette lighter concealed in the middle. *Why hadn;t anyone else noticed it? Or, had someone hidden it, after stealing it?*

While he was examining it, the old mechanic, Saa, came into the washsite to help him.

"That was Mr. Warner's. It has DW on the side!" He always carried it because he smoked a lot."

Howard looked at the lid and saw the DW.

Howard was astounded. *What didit mean? How long had it been in the Brough and how had it finished up there?*

"I suppose Mr. Warner gave it to Mr. Adams," Howard said. Suddenly, he had an idea. "Saa. Did Mr. Warner wear a ring?"

Saa thought for a moment. "Yes. He had a small ring on his little finger. It had a small garnet set in it. Mr. Warner found the garnet when he was washing samples and got a local goldsmith to make a ring for it."

Howard decided to keep this discovery to himself until he had more information.

He was made Security Officer in Charge, and given a raise in pay. A young Briton, Graham Byfield, who was twenty years old was sent to him to be trained as a DIASA security officer. Previously, he had worked in Banbury. One of his jobs had been as a guard at one of David Warner's appartment blocks in Banbury.

Tom Gough gave his mechanic two weeks off, so he could finish repairing the Brough. Howard had received expensive parts to replace the worn out and corroded ones. He was given permission to send it to England in the Cessna airplane when it went for its airworthyness certificate. Howard was very pleased he didn't have to send it by cargo ship with all the necessary paperwork and expense. He knew he could trust the pilot to deliver it to the DIASA store building in Banbury. He sent a letter, via the pilot, to Jean, asking her to buy new tires for the motorcycle and arrange for it to be spray painted.

Howard noticed Tamba Suluku was again driving one of the company's trucks. He heard from Leila, who still cleaned his house, that the clerk Tambafrom the old mine was now living in Paris.

Bob Taylor came to his office to tell him he was going to England with Abdul at the end of November for Mark Buzzard's inquest. "Unfortunately, you'll have to go to Conakry by Guinea Airways, via Kissidougou, because the Cessna won't be back by then. It'll be an interesting experience for you. By the way, the Banbury office says you can have the knife and the ring you found in that pit."

In early November, Howard sent the Brough to Matakourou in a lorry so it could be loaded into the Cessna for its trip to England. He put a personal note in the toolbox for Jean. He went with the lorry and wished he could have gone with the aircraft, but knew the company would not allow it. He thanked the pilot and engineer for taking the motorcycle. Afterwards the lorry returned to Banam.

Howard was invited to Abdul and Jeanine's for dinner. As usual, it was a very good meal cooked by the hostess. During the after dinner conversation, Jeanine mentioned she would love to go to England with Abdul. On the spur of the moment, Howard invited Abdul and her to stay with he and Jean if they went to England.

"Thanks," Jeanine said. "I'd love to, if I can find some way to go."

Bob and Angeline Taylor were also at the party. "I'll try to get DIASA to pay for Jeanine's flight," Bob said. "There's no reason why they shouldn't."

CHAPTER 20

O N THE TWENTIETH of November Howard, Abdul, Jeanine and
a driver set out in a Landrover for Kissidougou. Howard was very
excited because he was going to England and would see Jean again.
Abdul drove with Jeanine, sitting in the middle seat. The driver sat in the back,
but would have the vehicle to himself when he returned from the airport. The
return trip would be profitable if h could pick up some paying passengers.
Howard was only taking the small leather bag for his short stay. Jean had sent
a letter, agreeing to accommodate Adbdul and Jeanine. She also promised to
come out to the mine for two weeks when they returned.

Kissidougou airport was crowded, but Abdul knew how to cut through
red tape, and arrange things. So after an hour they were on the Antonov
plane for Conakry. Howard thought it looked more like a seaplane than a
landplane. The flight seemed to take about two hours by the time they got
off in Conakry. A company van took them to the Gbessia hotel. Howard had
a pleasant stay and a good dinner. Howard didn't stay up late. He wanted to
get some sleep before he arrived in England.

The next morning, he was awake at six o' clock and had his breakfast at
seven. He met the Kourouma's at breakfast. The flight to Paris was comfortable,
but Howard resented the time it took. He only started relaxing when he
arrived at Heathrow Airport in London. There, he had to wait for Abdul
and Jeanine while their Guinean, passports were checked by the Immigration
Service.

Eventually, they arrived at the exit barrier for the Arrivals Lounge. Jean and two of her brothers were there to meet them After many hugs and kisses, they went outside to the waiting cars.

"You must want to have a rest? so Tom and I will drive," Harry said.

"If you go with Tom, we'll go with Harry," Jean said.

After getting into the two cars, they were off on the road to Banbury and the motorway. Howard leaned against Jean in the back and went to sleep. He was awoken when they reached his house.

Jean had the spare room ready for the Kourouma's. "The inquest doesn't start till the day after tomorrow. So we can have a quiet day in Banbury tomorrow. Would you like something to drink?"

Everyone finished up drinking cocoa.

Jeanine, by request, cooked some French omelettes for breakfast. After a brief visit to the DIASA office and the stores depot they spent a leisurely day walking around Banbury. Ever practical Jeanine, bought some underclothes for herself and Abdul. "They gave me some English money at the office," she told Jean.

Howard was pleased to see the Woolpack still did lunches. He was worried about taking Abdul into a pub, but Abdul calmed his fears by drinking a cider with his meal. Jeanine had a small glass of Beaujolais wine. David Rhys joined them at the Woolpack. Howard was pleased to learn that the business was getting more profitable with the increased recruitment for DIASA. They did most of the initial checking up on job applicants for the company. Howard told David about some new ideas he had for the company and asked him to evaluate their profitability. One of the ideas he liked was getting into the house security sector.

They went back to the house for afternoon tea. In the evening they had a more formal meal at the Whately Hotel. Several of the office staff came to what turned out to be a pleasant evening. Afterwards, Howard, Jean and their guests were all tired so went home in a taxi.

The next morning, after a hearty breakfast cooked by Howard the two men set out along the road to Oxford. The two women stayed in Banbury.

"I'm glad Jean and Jeanine get on so well together," Howard said.

"Yes, I think Jeanine has found a friend. They're of a similar age, are both pregnant and have similar interests. It must be difficult sometimes for Jeanine being married to an African," Abdul replied.

"We're very pleased to have you here. Jean has even been talking about coming back to Banam with me for Christmas."

"Obviously, we'll be there for Christmas. But we may return here. DIASA has told The Ministry of Mines in Conakry they would like to have a Guinean working in their Banbury office. I've told them I'm interested in the job and have a very good chance of getting it. The government has to make a decision."

"You don't think they'll refuse?"

"No. It's too good an opportunity to promote Guinea. But they might take some time deciding."

When they arrived in the suburbs of Oxford, Howard put the Rover in a car park and they took a double-decker bus into the centre of the city.

"It's more convenient to park on the outskirts of the city and much less expensive," he told Abdul on the way. "We can walk from here."

At the central court building, he searched for the coroner's courtroom. "Oh, room 116," he said, when he had found it on the entrance board.

It was 9:20 a.m. and the court commenced at 9:30am. There weren't many people in the room, but Howard did recognised David Warner and waved to him.

The Coroner was sitting alone behind a barrier on a raised platform.

He started by saying the post morten examination had been performed and Mark Buzzard had been cremated. "Today, we will hear from Mr. Howard Evans and Mr. Abdul Kourouma who took statements from witnesses in Guinea, West Africa. Mr. Evans would you like to begin by telling us what happened from the time you arrived at the river."

Howard was impressed by the coroner knowing of the journey from Matakourou.

He told him about finding Buzzard's body.

"So, you didn't suspect he'd been attacked at first?"

"No. I just thought he'd wandered off the path and fallen down the hole. That was until I heard Tamba had sold some diamonds for him."

"Yes. The diamonds would provide a very good motive. Have any more diamonds turned up?"

"Not as far as we know," Howard said.

"I think we'll ignore the diamonds and concentrate on Mr. Buzzard's death. So, it could have been an accident?"

"That's possible."

The questioning carried on until one o' clock. The coroner ordered a recess for lunch. Howard took Abdul to a pub for lunch. They both had fish and chips, and sweet cider. Howard thought the afternoon session in Oxford was very boring and was very pleased when they arrived back in Banbury. That evening, they had a family dinner at Jean's sister's house. When they arrived home and were drinking coffee, Jean had news.

"We've been invited to afternoon tea at Rory Adams' sister's place. Heather lives in Chipping Warden which is about six miles away. I got the address from the DIASA office. I told her you had repaired the Brough Superior motorcycle and she said she'd like to see it. We're invited at three o' clock because I told her the headlight of the motorcycle wasn't working and you'd want to get back before dark. We can go in the car and you two men or just Howard can go on the bike. What do you think?"

"I'm willing to go on the motorcycle. It's ready now," Howard said quickly. "The headlight doesn't work. I've not got round to fixing it yet. But we can go early before it gets dark."

"I don't mind riding as a passenger," Abdul said. "It will be an unusual experience."

"I've often wondered what kind of family Rory came from," Jeanine said, "and now I shall find out."

"Yes, that story about his trying to take the diamonds to Sierra Leone always had an element of bravery and pathos about it. I always imagined a comfortable, middle class family setting. So, I'm not surprised he came from somewhere like Chipping Warden. I imagine Fiona, the judge's wife, came from a similar background."

The group carried on the conversation until Jean suggested it was getting late and they went to bed.

The next day, the men went to Oxford again. For some reason, Howard found the proceedings boring and was glad when the inquest was over. The Coroner gave an open verdict, and said "Mark Buzzard's death was caused by a fall into a stone lined pit."

Howard was very pleased when it was all over and they were back in Banbury.

On Saturday afternoon, he and Abdul rode the Brough Superior out to Chipping Warden. They had borrowed helmets from Jean's brothers. Howard drove very slowly because he wasn't used to riding a machine as large as a Brough. He took the road past the railway station and the cattle market and along to Kalibargo hill. The name had always intrigued him, but he had heard the tale of the Italian jeweler who had been murdered by his nephew on the hill. He would have let Abdul drive, but didn't know if his Guinea licence was valid in England. He decided to ask at the police station in Banbury. The two wives went in the Rover. Howard drove through Wardington village to show Abdul the cotswold stone houses. They stopped in the village and walked along the street. As they walked along Jean explained to Jeanine what an English tea was.

When they arrived in the village of Chipping Warden, the two women waited for their husbands in the car near the old church. Jeanine was intrigued by the truncated market cross, with the steps leading up to it.

"A town with the name Chipping was a market town. The Warden is something to do with a lookout hill, though the locals say it meant that there was a badger's den up there."

When the men arrived, they all drove along a narrow lane to a large Cotswold stone house.

Heather Bagley was sitting on a wooden bench in her garden. By her appearance, she was about sixty years old. She was dressed in a heavy tweed skirt and pink woolen cardigan. When she heard the vehicles, she came and opened a small gate at the side of the house. "Was that Rory's machine?" she asked.

"Yes. I've had it restored," Howard replied.

"It looks like it looked when Rory had it," she said.

"Thanks," Howard replied.

But Heather didn't examine the motorcycle. "Come in," she said, abruptly. Howard had the feeling that she wished they hadn't come. He presumed she didn't want to be reminded of Rory's death after all these years. She opened the front door and they went along a hallway into a small sitting room overlooking the garden. The room was simply furnished with armchairs and small tables. Howard noticed a large oil painting over the fireplace. It was a painting of the large hill overlooking Banam. He wondered if Rory Adams had painted it. He decided he wouldn't ask about it. Feeling out of place in this type of situation.

"My husband had to go out," she said, "some urgent business."

"What a delightful house," Jeanine exclaimed, "Have you lived here for a long time?"

"We bought it during the war. My husband was in the army and I wanted to make a nice home for him to return to. The money we got from Rory's insurance paid for it."

The tea, consisting of sandwiches, fruit, cakes, soft drinks and tea, was laid out on plates on top of a sideboard. "Help yourself," Heather said, pointing to the sideboard. The Banbury group helped themselves to the food and poured out a cup of tea each. Howard noticed Heather only took a cup of tea. Heather motioned them to sit in the chintz covered armchairs with the small side tables. "Please sit down."

Everyone sat.

"Someone inquired about Rory a few months ago. A man named Buzzard. I phoned David Warner, who's a friend of my husband, to see if he was genuine, and he confirmed he was legitimate. He had just got a job with DIASA, had heard the story about Rory and wanted to visit the old mine."

"That's surprising. Did you know Buzzard was found dead near the river some weeks ago?" We're here for the inquest which has just finished. It was held in Oxford."

Heather seemed interested in this information.

"How did he die?"

"The coroner recorded it as an accident."

"I'm interested because I showed Buzzard a copy of Rory's last letter which was written the day he died."

"What did he say?"

"Most of it was about when we were children and used to play games. He must have been homesick and thinking about when we were children playing in the vicarage garden. Our father was the vicar here before the war. We used to live in the old vicarage, a huge barracks of a building, which is near the church on the main road. In the old days, my father entertained the county set and gave them dinners. We children used to have to play with any youngsters who came, mainly at the weekend. We used to hide things in the garden and the other players had to find them from clues we left around."

"What sort of clues?"

"Sometimes we would use stones arranged as directional arrows. Sometimes we would mark trees with ribbons, or leave coins near the hidden object. To confuse the others, I would mark a small tree and leave the object under the largest tree near to it. Buzzard seemed very intrigued by this. I'll make a copy for you if you like?"

"Yes, if you could leave it at the Banbury office."

"I'll do it tomorrow. But I must leave now. I have a Parish meeting."

"One quick question." Howard asked, "Did Rory own a silver flask?'

"Yes. I gave it to him on his eighteenth birthday. We were at my grandfather's house in Dublin. It was expensive and took most of my pocket money for a year."

"I think I know where it is," Howard said.

"I'm not interested in getting it back. It was a gift to Rory and Rory died forty years ago. I'm amazed at how much interest there is in the account of Rory's last journey. But I must go now." She shook hands all round and they all went outside.

As they set off from the house, Howard said to Jean, "Follow us. I'd like to see the old vicarage garden if I can."

It was only a short distance away and luckily the house was empty because it had a *For Sale* notice by the entrance. They left the vehicles along the lane at the back of the house, opened the gate and went inside. A large stone wall surrounded the property. At the back of the house, there was an overgrown vegetable garden. They carried on along a stone path to the front of the house. The house was very large, with bay windows overlooking a large lawn. This had been recently cut and Howard smelled the new mowed grass. Near the stone wall along the main road, there were large trees and a rockery with a moss—encrusted fountain. One tree had a peculiar shape that looked familiar. It was a thick tree that six feet above the ground, split into two branches. Howard could see it would make an ideal place to hide things. As he and Jean walked around the house hand-in—hand to the garden, he remarked, "Wouldn't it make a wonderful place to bring up children? If I can ever afford it, I'll buy a place like this one day."

He decided he would find out how much they wanted for it before he left for Guinea.

Suddenly he was struck with an idea. The tree resembled one he had noticed in the patch of forest near the Kulu River, in Guinea. He wondered if Buzzard had noticed the resemblance? *Had he ever seen the tree in Chipping Warden?* He then realized that David Warner would have known about it. But, his thoughts were interrupted.

"Jeanine and I would like to attend a church service tomorrow, if possible. I've never been to a Church of England church," Abdul stated.

"We could come here tomorrow. The service starts at 10:30am. We'll come in the car,"

Howard replied. "When I was a child in Wales, I used to go to the Church of Wales services."

"I'll come," Jean said. This surprised Howard because he knew Jean wouldn't normally attend a non-Catholic service.

The ride back to Banbury was noisy and Howard speeded up as much as he could on the winding, country road past the fields and farms.

It was still light as they drove past Chacombe just outside Banbury. Howard decided to show them the lovely Cotswold stone house owned by David Warner. It was on the outskirts of the village; a large house, surrounded by lawns and trees. When they stopped for a few minutes, they could see the house in the distance with whisps of smoke rising from a stone chimney. It looked so peaceful. Howard didn't say anything, but contrasted it in his thoughts with the small thatched huts, in Guinea. He was shocked by his attitude. As an ex-policeman, he considered himself cynical about people's ways of acquiring wealth. Years later, he realized this was the occasion when he finally decided he couldn't carry on with his DIASA job.

Later that evening, when they were sitting around after dinner Jean brought up the subject of Rory's flask. "Do you think Mark Buzzard found Rory's flask near the river?"

"It's a possibility. I think that's where Rory hid the diamonds. Who knows?" Abdul said.

"If he did, Tom Gough must have them now," Howard said, with conviction.

"But he always strikes me as being such an ineffectual person," Jeanine said, yawning. "I'm ready for bed."

"He may have struck it rich when he teamed up with Leila. Tamba Suluku must have told him about the diamonds. I wonder if that's the answer—Leila, Suluku and Tom? Anyway, we won't solve it tonight so let's go to bed," Howard said.

The next day, they drove up Kalabargo hill and over the county border into Northamptonshire. It was a dry, cold day, with a timid sun that didn't give much heat. In Chipping Warden, they turned right just after the bus shelter, before the famous ancient tree and along a walled lane. They parked along this road and walked into the side door of the church. The church was very old and built of a soft cotswold stone. Howard led the way and sat in a pew on the rightside. He wondered what Abdul, a Muslim, would think of the small village congregation. Abdul didn't say anything. Luckily, the hymns were some of Howard's favourites. The vicar's sermon was based on loving one's neighbours. At the end of the morning service, some people left and the rector started the communion service.

"Do you want to stay?" Howard asked the others.

"Yes, I think it will be interesting," Abdul said. The others concurred, politely.

Howard was the only one of the quartet to go to the communion rail and take communion.

While he was drinking the wine from the cup, he noticed the initials DW in a diamond shape on the base. It was similar to the initials on the cigarette lighter he had found in the toolbox of the Brough. In the centre of the diamond shape was a shiny, dark, green stone that looked like a piece of glass.

When the group was saying goodbye to the rector, he asked. "I was impressed with the wine goblet at the communion today. Is it very old?"

"No, not really. A Mr. Warner gave it to the church in 1950 as a memorial to his friend Rory Adams. Mr. Adams sister still lives in the village. He was killed in West Africa during the war. The stone in the base is actually a boart diamond."

Howard wondered if David Warner had given the church the gift in atonement for a great sin, but doubted he would ever find the truth.

They walked along to the Griffen pub for a beer and then drove back to Banbury.

On Monday, Howard drove down to Wales with his wife and guests. He enjoyed the next few days showing the Kouroumas some of his favourite spots. The time passed much too quickly.

CHAPTER 21

AT THE END of the next week on December 9th., they were on the plane travelling back to Guinea. Howard considered the pleasant time he'd had travelling with the Kouroumas and his wife. This second trip from England to Conakry was more pleasant than the first. The main difference was he was travelling with his wife and friends. Also, he knew what conditions were like in Banam and wouldn't be shocked this time. He tried to tell Jean what to expect, but found it hard to convey the atmosphere there. He hoped she wouldn't be too disappointed with conditions there, and that it didn't affect her health. However Jean had insisted on coming.

The Kourouma's spent Saturday night with friends in Conakry while Howard and Jean stayed at the Independence Hotel. Jean was impressed with the food and service. The Cessna met them at the airport and Jean wasequally impressed that they would be travelling in the company plane. The trip to Matakourou passed without incident. Jean was intrigued with the small African villages they saw on the way.

Jean and Howard stayed with the McVeigh's in Matakourou. Jean admired their large house with its solid furniture. When they were in bed later that night she told Howard she thought she would have a good holiday here. "If the accommodation in Banam is like here I shall be happy."

Howard tried to tell her what Banam was like, but realized she would have to experience it herself.

The trip to Banam in a Landrover fatigued her and Howard wondered if it had been sensible for her to travel out to Guinea. She assured him she was alright and would be fine by the next day. His living accommodation, however, seemed shocking to her after the Matakourou houses.

"Surely, they could have found better prefabricated buildings than these containers?" she said.

"They're only supposed to be a short-term solution," Howard replied.

"Uh," she snorted. "Even you can't believe that. But I'm glad I came. I've never been anywhere like Guinea."

"We've been invited to dinner tonight. Jeanine and Abdul are preparing a dinner in the club. Do you want to skip it?"

"Certainly not. I want to meet all the people you've decribed."

The dinner was a great success.

Howard was pleased she had come, but was dreading when she went back to England after Christmas.

The first day, he went to work at his office. After Hardwright had gone back to Matakourou, he told Bob Taylor he would like to look around the path where Buzzard died, as he had new information. Bob readily agreed and walked along with him. This time, they concentrated on a large tree that one of the older workers had told Howard had always been there. It didn't take long to find the small hole in the rock under the tree roots where the flask might have been hidden.

"Everybody was looking in the wrong place," Bob said in amazement.

"Yes. Buzzard was the first person who thought of contacting Rory's sister. When he heard about their childhood games, he realized where the diamonds were hidden. But, we still don't know who has the diamonds now."

One evening, Howard decided to talk to Tom Gough. Jean and Jeanine had gone to visit some friends.

When he walked over to his house he noticed only Tom's vehicle outside. But he heard voices and laughter coming from inside the house. When he knocked, the door was opened by Tom.

"Come in. Come in. I've got company."

He went inside. The small space was crowded. Tamba Suluku was sitting at the table, drinking a beer. His wife, Leila, and her sister were sitting on the bed, drinking beers. Tom returned to his place near the table. "Would you like a beer?" he asked Howard.

"Yes, I'd like a beer." Howard replied, though he felt awkward because Tambas was there. "Would you like another, Tamba?" Tom asked Suluku.

As though sensing Howard's attitude, Suluku stood up and motioned Howard to take his place. "I must go," he said. "Thanks for the beer. I'm pleased to see you're back, Mr. Evans." He went outside and Howard heard him walk down the hill.

As the windows and the venetion blinds were closed, it was very hot inside the cabin. Tom was only wearing shorts. Leila and her sister were wearing short, brightly coloured dresses.

"Let's sit outside. It's too hot in here. Bring your beers."

They went outside under the straw roof and sat on canvas chairs. The women sat on a crudely made bench.

Tom asked Howard about his trip to England and the coroner's verdict.

"Oh, It went very well. You know the coroner returned an accidental death verdict?"

"I always thought it was an accident," Leila said. "Mr. Buzzard was very drunk that night."

Then the conversation changed. Tom was worried about his medical examination in London when he went on leave at the end of the year. "I don't know what I'm going to do if DIASA fires me. I've been living in Africa since I left the navy in 1946. I feel like an alien when I go to England these days. It's changed so much. I miss the climate and the people here. Normally, I stay in the same small hotel in London. It's quite comfortable. You get a small kitchen with your room, so I can cook my own meals. But I'm always so pleased to come back here. "

"You'll soon get used to it," Howard said. "There are plenty of part time jobs you can get. I'm sure DIASA will help you get a job. You could work in their stores in Banbury."

"Yes. I suppose I'm too pessimistic. But I'm going to miss the life out here and the Africans."

"That's why I think you should try to get a job with DIASA in Banbury. That way you could possibly get trips out here."

Howard finished his beer, refused another one and walked down the road. As he left, he looked back toward the house and saw Tom and the women carrying their beers into the house. Tom seemed happy tonight and the women were obviously happy in his company. He thought it was too hot to hurry, so he walked slowly back to his cabin. He couldn't remember why he had wanted to speech to Tom. He collected a cold beer from inside the refrigorator, sat outside and drank it.

Jean returned from her appointment and cooked their dinner. When they had finished the meal, they went to bed early.

The three weeks Jean lived in Banam were very satisfying. Jean was well liked by the local people who gave her gifts of food they grew and local artefacts such as pottery basketwork and carvings. Jean always gave things in return. Howard was perturbed by the amount of clothes she gave away and worried that the local people were taking advantage of her. But she reassured him, "I shall have to get new clothes after the baby comes."

"But most of the clothes were bought for you to wear here."

"Yes. That's true. But it's easier for me to buy new clothes in England than these people in Guinea. Anyway, they can't afford good clothes with the money they're paid. It's the least I can do to help them."

Leila's sister, Fatima, worked for Jean and finished up with a box of clothing.

Jean and Howard went out to people's houses, or the club almost every night. They attended a very formal Christmas party at Matakourou and a very informal Boxing day party at Banam. Jean had brought a lot of presents for Howard's friends and the Guinean children at Banam.

Howard illustrated the plight of the local people by telling her the story of the cats the expatriates kept in the kitchen. "We fed the cats with sardines because the company didn't import cat food. Then we noticed the cats were getting thinner and found out the night watchman was taking the sardines for his children. That kind of thing makes me feel that we could do more for these people. Though we do provide them with basic foods like rice and cooking oil."

One Sunday morning, Jean asked Howard to take her to the old village because she had arranged to photograph some of the children. "The children would love to have their photos taken and it will give me some souvenirs for my album."

After breakfast, Howard and his wife walked down to the old village ten minutes away from their house. The village had been there for years and it was about half a mile from the river. The villagers grew crops such as rice vegatables and a kind of millet. Suluku's father, also called Suluku and just as ugly as his son, was the witchdoctor there.

DIASA wasn't too happy about the village being in its lease area, but it did provide a source of labour to the company.

When they arrived the whole village turned out to welcome them. Howard had arranged for a security driver to bring his Landrover, with cases of soda and packets of chocolate biscuits. The ayor of the village made a speech to the crowd and one of his wives showed Jean the inside of his large house. Jean took photographs of his family and house.

Then, it was Suluku's turn. He put on his devil's costume of grass stalks and bells and Jean photographed him dancing. Afterward she had to photograph all the children, one-by-one. Luckily, she had brought plenty of film. Some of the young children, about six years old, insisted on being photographed carrying large buckets of water. Jean promised to send everybody copies of their photographs. On the journey back to their house in the Landrover, Jean was sad. "I feel the company could do more to help those people. Why don't they put in a water supply?"

"The people could do it themselves, you know. The company is worried that if they start handing out things, they'll finish up with half of Guinea on their doorstep. It's one of the reasons we don't give free medical treatment to everyone, only DIASA employees."

"I still think it's wrong."

Howard thought it was wise to say no more.

Jean's vacation in Guinea passed much too quickly for Howard. Just before the New Year, she returned to England. Howard was pleased Tom Gough was travelling with her. Howard travelled to Matakourou with Jean. Tom was waiting at the airport with Leila. Howard spoke to Tom before he left and wished him well. He was surprised by how happy Tom looked, considering he had been worrying about his forthcoming medical examination in London—followed by possible dismissal. But Howard surmised he was happy to be going to England.

Howard assured Jean he would arrive in England before the birth of their child.

CHAPTER 22

*A*FTER JEAN LEFT, Howard felt very lonely. After work, he spent the next two evenings in his cabin. He had videos, that Jean had brought with her, showing himself, Jean and her family together over the months he had known them. He viewed them time and time again.

Jean had been gone three days when he heard a rumour about Tom Gough. One of the arriving passengers from England heard from the Banbury office that Tom Gough had died. He couldn't believe it because it said Tom had died in London on the day he arrived.

The passenger brought a letter from Jean. She wrote, *Tom Gough dropped dead of a heart attack just after Nick, my cousin, picked me up for the journey back to Banbury.*

I was in a hurry to get home and left Tom in the baggage retrieval hall. He wasn't in a hurry because he was staying in a hotel near the airport. I gave him a hug and a kiss because he looked so lonely. On the plane, he told me they were going to do some stress tests at a private hospital in Richmond. I'll write to you again when I hear more news.

When he told the men in the club at Banam, he found they weren't too interested and seemed to know already. News, especially bad news, seemed to travel fast in West Africa.

When he received Jean's next letter, it was dated January 8th. *Apparently Tom had a heart attack after he left the customs area at the Airport. A policeman tried to give him mouth to mouth and a doctor arrived with oxygen, but he must have had a massive heart attack and died instantly.*

He was cremated yesterday at Redditch. I'm not quite sure why he was cremated there, but DIASA may have an interest in the crematorium. Only David Warner and me were there. Tom's brother lives in Adelaide, Australia and will get the insurance money. Mr. Warner drove me down there in his Mercedes.

The service was very nice, but rather sad. Tom must have felt very alone here in England. He couldn't have had many friends. Otherwis, they would have come to the service. All his friends must have been in Africa. They have a lift that takes the coffin from the chapel down into the furnace. You can feel the immense heat coming up. The whole thing was very efficient. I had lunch with Mr. Warner afterwards. He asked me to dispose of Tom's ashes. He suggested that I take them out to sea and drop them overboard, as Tom was a sailor at one time. I've decided to take a day trip to France and empty the box into the sea from the ferry. The rest of her news was about her family and endearments.

Her next letter described how she had taken a day trip from Dover to Calais and thrown the ashes, over the side of the boat about half-way across. *I kept the original lacquered box as a souvenir. It was very choppy, coming back and I was quite sick.*

The next news that interested Howard was of an attempted coup in Conakry. It interested him because he was in Conakry at the time. He'd delivered a diamond shipment to the government office in Conakry and afterwards had been driven to the Gbessia Hotel. He was to return to the mine the next day with Nicole Andrews who had just arrived on the plane from England. The girl was eighteen years old, slim with attractive blonde hair. She went to her room after she arrived and stayed there. Her father, Albert, was one of the construction foremen helping to build the Matakourou camp. The pilot of the DIASA plane was also staying at the hotel. The Gbessia was smaller and cheaper than the Independence and he presumed the company was trying to save money by sending him there.

In the evening, he was drinking beer in the bar with the pilot, when they heard gunfire coming from the army camp that was behind the hotel. A very scared Nicole, dressed in shorts and a Tee-shirt, ran into the room and sat near Howard.

"What the hell's that?" the pilot asked. They didn't have long to wait before they found out.

Minutes later, a group of dishevelled, sweating soldiers, carrying AK 47 automatic rifles ran into the bar. Some were dressed in their uniforms. Some were not wearing their shirts. "We want whiskey," they shouted.

The Guinean barman refused. "You can only have drinks if you pay for them," he explained in a calm voice. Howard admired his courage, though he thought it bordered on insanity considering the circumstances. The soldiers looked as if they were going to help themselves anyway. Luckily for the barman, an officer arrived and ordered the men out of the hotel. The radio behind the bar had been turned on and the Conakry station broadcast an announcement in French. "This is the Guinea Revolutionary Government. We have taken over. Remain calm and stay in your houses. No one will be harmed."

Howard's French was not brilliant, but he understood the gist of the announcement. The message was broadcast continously over the next two hours. Then, it stopped abruptly, and the station played African music.

Later, the station broadcast an announcement saying an attempted coup had been suppressed and the previous government was back in control. He heard gunfire from the army camp, but realized the soldiers were only celebrating their successful supression of the revolt by firing their rifles into the air.

Nicole was very reluctant to go to her room. "I'm worried someone might try to come in during the night,"

Howard eventually persuaded her there was no danger. She was so tired, she went to bed.

He and the pilot carried on, drinking till about eleven o' clock and before going to their bedrooms.

The pilot, Nicole and Howard met again and had breakfast together the next morning. The Guinean co-pilot arrived in a taxi and went with the pilot to the airport. Later, they returned to the hotel to announce they would not be leaving that day. Howard and Nicole spent a pleasant day, swimming in the pool and sunbathing. Nicole looked particularly attractive in her brief bikini. He hoped Jean had not heard about the coup.

The next morning, the pilot told him that they had authority to leave Conakry. Howard, Nicole and two other passengers went to the airport in a small bus. The flight to Matakourou was very smooth and Howard was glad to be back in the DIASA lease. Nicole was met by her parents but did give Howard a grateful kiss before she left.

Howard received a very worried letter from Jean later in the week. He had already written her a letter about his stay in Conakry.

Jeanine and Abdul left for England in February. Howard organized a party for them in the Banam club. He was very sorry to see them go because he was so used to visiting them in the evenings. But he was glad because they would be company for Jean and a sort of link between Banbury and Banam.

Chapter 23

*H*OWARD HAD NOT seen Nicole again, except casually when he went to Matakourou. He was very surprised when he went to the club one Saturday at lunchtime and saw her there.

"I'm staying with the Taylors for a few days. I came with Mrs. Taylor yesterday evening."

"You'll find Banam very different from Matakourou. It might be too quiet for you. Would you like a drink?"

"A beer, please." Nicole smiled, showing her even teeth. "I think I'm going to enjoy my visit to Banam."

Howard went into the bar and came out with two beers. He was flattered by the girl's obvious interest in him. Also, he was bored and welcomed someone new to talk to. "You can have lunch here if you like," he said. "I normally do, on at weekends."

"I'd like that."

Howard enjoyed his lunch with Nicole. Mrs. Taylor came in, but left when she saw Nicole was being entertained by Howard.

During lunch, Nicole told Howard she would like to climb up to the top of the flat-topped hill. "I've looked at it every morning from Matakourou. It dominates the countryside like a forbidding, hostile castle and I'd like to stand on top like a crusading knight and survey the plains below."

"I'm not too sure if anyone will want to climb to the top again. We did it a few weeks ago. But, I'll take you. The exercise will do me good."

"As long as it's no trouble."

"No. It's no trouble. We'll make it into an interesting trip. We'll have lunch in the shade at the bottom of the hill. Then, in the afternoon, we can climb the hill. I'll see if anyone else wants to go."

"I'm glad you've got someone young and pretty to talk too," Bob Taylor said, enigmatically.

Early the next morning, Howard and Nicole set out from the club in Howard's Landrover.

As he had thought, no one else was keen to climb the hill on what looked like a hot, humid day.

Jeffrey Ellis, who seemed to like Nicole, had prepared a cold box full of fruit, vegetables and salads and another one with meats for the barbeque. Jeanine had provided a grill and some charcoal.

"This is fun," Nicole said, as they set off.

Howard thought she seemed like a young girl on vacation from a strict private school—savouring her freedom. She looked particularly attractive in her brief, white shorts and tee shirt. Though after a few miles on the red laterite road, he knew the shorts wouldn't be white for too long. He was wearing khaki shorts and a blue, cotton shirt.

As they drove along, the road the temperature became hotter and hotter in the Landrover. The heat seemed attracted to the aluminium roof. The cab inside heated to the temperature of a Turkish bath. The dust kicked up by the wheels blew into the cab, sticking to their hot, sweating bodies. Howard regretted coming, but Nicole didn't seem too upset by the heat and dust.

"I'm sorry it's such an oppressive day," he said, wiping the sweat from his forehead with his hand.

"I'm glad I came," she said, placing her cool hand on his sweating, left thigh.

He couldn't understand how her hand was so cool. He found it very soothing. Later when she squeezed his thigh higher up, he realized Nicole had misconstrued his interest in her. He was unsure how to dissuade her from escalating their relationship without upsetting her—or even if he wanted to. He decided to do nothing. Luckily, he didn't have to make a decision. They quickly arrived at the bottom of the hill.

Howard suggested that they climb the hill first and have their meal when they returned.

"I've been told there's a very nice, warm pool in a cave on the other side," she said.

"Yes. I've heard that story. But no one seems to have found it. We'll look after lunch."

He parked the Landrover under a shady tree and they got out.

"I'll take a couple of beers. The track is to the right," he said, leading the way.

As they were both very fit, the walk to the top was not too difficult.

When they reached the top, Nicole walked around looking for the best viewpoint. "I can see Matakourou over there."

"Yes. You can see for miles from here." Howard removed his small knapsack and put it on the ground. Then he removed his wet shirt and spread it over a small bush. He was surprised when Nicole removed her tee shirt and bra and hung them over a bush. Her body was firm and tanned.

"There's no one up here and it's such a good opportunity to cool off."

"It doesn't bother me. Let's drink the beer before it gets too hot."

The sight of the partially clothed young woman made him feel uncomfortable, though he couldn't think why it should. Perhaps his ideas of morality and conduct learned from his grandmother, were too out of date.

There wasn't much shade on top of the hill, but they found a small shrub to sit under and drink the beer. Howard leaned against the tree trunk and Nicole sat between his legs, leaning against him.

"My God, it's hot up here," she said running the cold tin of beer over her stomach and under her breasts. She turned sideways and rubbed the tin across Howard's stomach. He could feel the weight of her moist, warm breast against his chest and arm, the silky smoothness of her leg over his. She leaned against him. He knew she could tell he was aroused. When he didn't move or touch her she ressumed her former position.

After finishing the beers, they picked up their clothes. Nicole pulled her tee-shirt over her head and Howard put his shirt in the rucksack. They walked down the path to the Landrover.

On the way down, they stopped to examine a huge ant hill. It looked about fifteen foot tall like a cairn in the Scottish highlands made of a concrete-like clay. There were thousands of ants running around. It looked out of place on this grassy hillside.

At the bottom, they built a small barbeque pit with some stones they found, filled it with charcoal and put the grill on top.

After eating a well-cooked meal and having two more beers, Howard felt satiated. Nicole decided she would like to find the pool she's been told about. "Let's try to find the pool. I feel like a dip."

They repacked the Landrover and put out the fire.

"It has to be behind those trees to the left of the track," Howard said. "I noticed a water course down the hill when we came last time. It must disappear for most of the year."

Nicole hurried around the corner and through the bamboo-like trees. Howard followed, but soon lost sight of her.

"There's a small opening here. It seems to go into the hill," he heard through the closely spaced trees. He followed the sound of her voice. She was standing in a small open space looking into a tall, narrow aperture between two tall rocks.

"I can smell sulphur," Nicole said, leaning forward and sniffing the air. "This must be the place."

"I'd better go inside first. You don't know what we might find. There could be animals or snakes." Howard eased himself slowly through the opening. He didn't want to cut himself on the rocks and hoped they wouldn't collapse.

Nicole followed closely, clutching the back of his shirt, he could feel her breath on the back of his neck.

Inside, he found himself in a large cave. It was dark inside, but became lighter when he and Nicole moved away from the entrance.

The floor was sandy. Along one wall of the cave was a small pool of water ten feet long and eight feet wide. The pool was steaming and emitting the sulphur smell.

"The Guineans say you can bathe in the water, if it's not too hot," she said, "Let's try it."

Howard noticed she stood back to let him test it. He put his hand in the pool. "It seems cool enough." he said, withdrawing his hand. He looked behind him and saw Nicole was already taking off her shoes. She seemed to be in a hurry and was soon completely naked. She looked at Howard who hadn't even taken off his shoes. "Well, are you coming in?' she asked, in a demanding tone.

Howard felt as though he was the pupil being compelled to do something for a demanding teacher. The fact that the teacher was younger than he, female and completely unclothed made it more bizzare to him. He didn't know what to say and found it disconcerting talking with an unclothed female who was not his wife.

Nicole dipped her foot in the water. Finding it cool enough, she then sat on the rocky edge and slowly entered the water. The water reached up to her shoulders and she floated away. "Come on in. It's invigorating." Her tone was more inviting.

Howard turned away from the pool and slowly took off his clothes. When he was down to his briefs, he stopped. They were the pair, decorated with flowers that Jean had bought for him in Banbury. He felt vulnerable without his clothes. He turned and gazed at Nicole floating in the pool. The water was clear and he could see Nicole's tanned body, every curve and indentation, from her head to her feet. It was very inviting. She used her arms to propel herself slowly across the pool.

He sat on the side of the pool, dangling his feet in the water. *No one would know,* he thought. He was very tempted, but Nicole spoiled the moment by speaking.

"Aren't you coming in?" she asked, again with a commanding tone.

"No. I've decided not to."

Suddenly he decided he wouldn't jeodize his marriage by indulging in a short, sexual adventure. Nicole now seemed like a piranha circling its prey. *Did she think he was an easy target?* Nicole walked toward him. Howard stood, dried himself on his shirt, put on his other clothes and walked away.

"Oh! Suit yourself. I just thought we could have fun together, but you are a bit of a misery. I'll come out."

She got out of the pool, dried herself and dressed. They walked back to the Landrover and drove back to Banam, without barely speaking.

"Thanks for taking me up the moutain," she said. "Your wife is a very lucky woman."

"See you around."

Shortly after their trip, she went back to England.

The rest of his time in Guinea passed rather quickly and he was eager to return to Banbury to witness the birth of his child. By April, he was ready to go back to England and was not thinking of returning to Guinea. When he packed, he took anything he wanted to keep.

CHAPTER 24

By APRIL, HOWARD was eager and impatient to return to Jean, and witness the birth of their child. Everything went well on his trip from Conakry, and he found himself at London Airport once again. Tom, Jean's brother, met him at the airport and drove him to Banbury.

Howard was dropped off at his house with his luggage. On the flight back to England, he'd decided he would not return to Guinea under any circumstances. However, he also decided not to tell Jean until he had secured another job. He hoped that they'd saved up enough money and the security firm could support him and his partner.

The next morning, along with Jean, he went to see David Rhys. The building was in Parsons Street. Jean wanted some exercise, so they walked down to the town. She went to her small office just inside the front door and Howard went to see David had an office on the second floor. David seemed pleased to see him and explained that business had picked up over the last six months, especially since they'd added the electronic alarm system line.

"We have a full-time employee fixing the systems now."

"So, you think the business could support both of us now?"

"Yes. With vetting new employees for DIASA and other companies and the electronic business, we may have to take on more employees."

"I'm glad to hear it because I don't want to go back to Guinea. I don't think I'm cut out to live in these out of the way places. I'd like to start in about two weeks time. If that's Okay with you.?"

"I've got your office ready for you and you could start tomorrow, if you want to."

"I'll just pop along and see the DIASA people to tell them I won't be going back. They've been fair to me and I want to tell them as soon as possible."

"I'll see you when you're ready then." David said.

As Howard passed the front desk, he kissed Jean and left.

From the office in Parsons Street, he walked along the road to the DIASA office. He felt he must tell them that he was not going back to Guinea. He saw Richard Compton's Jaguar parked outside the large house that had been converted into offices for DIASA. He was ushered into Richard Compton's office without delay. He told him of his decision not to go back to Guinea. "I've tried it for a year and don't think I can operate successfully in that kind of situation."

Richard Compton was very understanding. "Yes. I think in your circumstances, expecting a child, I would feel the same way. But, if you do change your mind and decide to return, we'll still find you a security job. Remember, you still have seven weeks paid leave coming to you. You don't have to decide till then. Afterwards, we'd like you to continue working for us for the time being. You can work from your office in Banbury, interviewing people for jobs in Guinea, vetting them from a security point of view and telling them what it's like out there. We'll work out details after your leave."

"That sounds like a great job. Thanks. I've enjoyed working for you, but I just thought I'd let you know so you could find someone else."

"That's very good of you. We'll look around and recruit someone, if you definitely don't want to go back. We can always send Abdul out as a temporary measure."

"Yes. He could do the job."

When he left the manager's office he walked along the corridor to Abdul's office, next door. Abdul was sitting behind his desk writing. He was pleased to see Howard. They spent a pleasant hour talking about Guinea and DIASA. The room had maps of the DIASA mine pinned to the walls. A Guinean antique rice god statue, decorated one of the shelves. Howard left feeling a little sad that he was leaving Guinea, even though he knew it was the right decision. On the way home he called in at Littlewoods, for a cup of coffee and a Banbury cake.

The next two weeks seemed to go quickly because Howard was busy. He spent time in his office with David Rhys, trying to understand how their business operated and waited for Jean to give birth. He sensed Jean was hiding something from him, but decided not to ask her what it was until the child was delivered.

One day sorting, through some of his personal papers he got a shock. While working in Guinea he didn't need much money for daily expenses and saved a lot. He had several savings accounts. One deposit account with a Danish Bank, paid a high rate of interest without deducting tax. This was allowable while he wasn't resident in England. He realized that as he was again a resident in Britain, he would have to pay tax on the interest. He found the pass book and looked at the balance. It was much higher than he remembered. When he looked at the last entry, he saw that ten thousand pounds had been deposited into the account in January. This puzzled him because he knew it must have been done by Jean. But, where had she got the money? He decided he wouldn't ask her about the deposit until after their child was born. He carefully searched through his desk to see if he could find deposit slips, or other papers, showing where the money had come from. He found nothing.

When he mentioned Tom Gough's death and Jean's disposal of his ashes, he thought Jean was deliberately vague about her trip to France. He decided not to upset her, and didn't pursue the matter. He had no idea what she could be hiding. However, he did not think too much about it over the next few weeks leading up to the birth of his son. Jean was only in the hospital for four days. There were no complications.

Howard did not find out Jean's secret till after the christening of his son, David Llewelyn.

For some reason, after the christening Jean wished to rid herself of a secret she had been hiding for several weeks. It was what Howard wished to know. She told him where the unknown money had come from. It was as though she wished to cleanse herself of some wrongdoing.

After the christening, when Howard and Jean were playing with the child she told him of something she had done while he was away. "Howard, there's something I should have told you when you came back from Guinea. But, I was cowardly because I knew you wouldn't approve, so I've just kept quiet. Recently, I've sensed you know something is wrong and I'm keeping something secret."

"I discovered you had deposited #10,000 into our bank account and wondered where the money came from?"

"I suspected you had found out somehow."

"It was accidental. I was wondering how much money we had saved from Guinea?"

"Well, it started with Tom's death. Only David Warner and I went to the crematorium service. Afterwards, Mr. Warner gave me Tom's ashes and asked me to scatter them. He said he would pay any expenses. The ashes were in a lacquered box."

"Why wouldn't Warner take the ashes? You were pregnant."

"He said he was too busy. Also, we were some of the only friends Tom had. So, I didn't mind. The Banbury office booked a day trip to Calais for me, as I decided to scatter his ashes at sea. I thought Tom would like that because he was a sailor during the war. I decided to go on the next Tuesday because it wouldn't be as busy as at the weekend or on a Monday. If I'd asked, some one would have gone with me but I didn't want anyone to lose a day's pay.

"Anyway, the box sat on the mantlepiece in the front room. I was looking at the box and became curious about the ashes inside. It sounds a bit morbid, but I couldn't imagine what human ashes looked like. I resisted the temptation to look inside for hours, but in the end I opened the lid. It had a little catch thing on it. I was disappointed at first because they just looked like the powdery ashes you get when you rake out a dead fire. Then I noticed a large piece of what at first I thought was a piece of bone. But I knew it wasn't because it was shaped like a large pea. I grabbed a pair of plastic gloves and picked it out of the box. It was dirty looking in the ashes, so I took it over to the sink and washed it under the tap. That's when I discovered it was a diamond. It had that unearthly inner fire. You could see the brilliance when it was wet. I was so amazed I nearly dropped it down the plug hole. I had to sit down and think about what it meant to us. I was shocked. *How did a diamond get mixed up with Tom's ashes?* I remembered Tom telling me that in Sierra Leone the IDM would keep their diamonds under their tongues and if necessary swallow them."

"It sounds a bit dangerous, swallowing diamonds?"

"No. You can do it easily. Especially if you put them in food. But, that wasn't my problem. I wondered if there were any more. I was worried that someone might come and see me. So, I took the ashes, a bucket of water, a flour sieve and a plastic bowl out to the garden shed. I used a watering can to wash the ashes through the sieve into the bowl."

"I find that a bit gruesome."

"Yes, it was. But remember, I was wearing a pair of rubber gloves."

"How many diamonds did you find?"

"Twenty."

"Twenty. What sort of sizes?"

"They varied. Most were like the first one, the size of a large pea."

"So that's where the #10,000 came from?"

"Yes. I sold two of the diamonds."

"How and where?" Howard knew he sounded like a policeman questioning a suspect, but couldn't change his tone of voice or attitude. His honest wife had turned into a thief. He didn't know what to do about it.

"I took them on my ferry trip to Calais. I stayed one night in London and scattered Tom's ashes on the sea from the boat. Then, I carried on to Calais."

"Wait a minute. Didn't you think of returning the diamonds to DIASA? They didn't belong to you."

"They didn't belong to anybody. I looked on them as a gift from God. I knew it was our escape from Guinea. After my trip out there, I didn't want you going back after David was born."

"Where did you sell the diamonds?"

"In Antwerp. When I arrived in Calais, I caught another train and carried on to Antwerp. I had heard you can sell diamonds there. It was so easy. I just went into a jewellers shop that had a notice in the window saying they bought diamonds, and said I had two rough diamonds to sell. It was quite simple and quick. He didn't ask where they came from, or how I got them. He offered to pay me in various ways and I chose American Express travellers cheques. We walked to a bank and he obtained the travellers cheques. It was then I realized I had done a stupid thing because I would have to sign my real name. I decided there was only a very small risk that someone would link these travellers cheques to diamonds. He said he'd buy any more diamonds I had."

Howard didn't know what to do. As an ex-policeman, he knew Jean shouldn't have taken the diamonds but didn't know how to correct the situation. He couldn't go to DIASA and tell them Tom had swallowed stolen diamonds, or that Jean had sorted through his ashes and found them. The whole story sounded bizarre. [*They might think he had stolen them. Where had the diamonds come from? Were they the lost cache from the old mine? Had Tom killed Buzzard to get them, or had he bought them from some of his African friends?*]

"What did you do with the other diamonds?"

"They're in the bank in Banbury. No one else knows about them."

Howard looked at his beautiful, young wife and thought how little he knew about her. He never thought she was capable of such an act. "You're amazing, Jean. I never thought you could do anything like this. I wish you waited till we discussed it."

Looking across the room, Howard was amazed that his simply dressed, attractive wife could do such an unethical act. He realized he did not know as much about her, as he had previously thought. He hoped he could quickly regain his former implicit trust in her.

"Howard, Remember, I didn't know Tom had swallowed the diamonds. I was only curious to see what human ashes looked like. But, when I found the diamonds, I realized they were ours. They didn't belong to anyone. Who did they belong to? The original diamond company? The French government? The Guinea government? No one was hurt by me taking them. They must be the ones from the old mine. The diamonds carried by Rory Adams. By now, they'd be classified as treasure trove."

"Yes. Tom must have found them, or taken them from Buzzard. I hope he didn't kill him to get them."

"That's another reason why I didn't take them to the office. I didn't want DIASA thinking Tom, though dead, was a thief, or that you stole them and I was making up this story—but for some reason changed my mind."

Howard sighed. "Yes, I can see you were in a difficult position and just did what you thought was best. I suppose you couldn't very well ask anyone for advice. We can't change anything now. We can use some of the money to do good. Possibly, we could use some to support African charities. Let's leave the diamonds where they are in the bank and only sell a couple every year. That way we shan't get rich too quickly."

Howard knew he was deceiving himself. He remembered his Grandmother's admonition, "Never lie to yourself." He could still return the diamonds and the money to DIASA in various ways. He just didn't want to suffer the any possible consequences.

Jean looked happier. "Yes, Dear. We'll only use the money if we need it. We could buy that house in Chipping Warden now, if it's still for sale."

Howard hoped he wasn't going to get any more unpleasant surprises in the near future. He supposed he should work on the Brough Superior. He needed to replace the headlights.

CHAPTER 25

$\mathcal{H}$OWARD SOON BECAME used to his new lifestyle. He preferred it to his former life as a police officer and most definitely to his life as a security officer in Guinea. He was happy most of the time. But he did have one niggling cause for unhappiness. He found it difficult to forgive Jean for acquiring the diamonds in such a disgusting manner. Sometimes, looking at her he imagined a harpy sorting through Tom's entrails. He knew he was being unworldly about her retrieval of the diamonds, but he'd expected her to have a higher moral standard. He knew it would have been difficult or impossible to return them to their rightful owners. *Who were the legal owners of the diamonds, anyway?* But he was so busy the diamonds soon faded in significance.

He and Jean were still very friendly with the Kouroumas, Abdul and Jeanine. They were buying a house in Sussex Drive and Howard was helping Abdul decorate it. Jean and Jeanine did the fabrics for the new house and babysat for each other. They were together very often.

Abdul and Howard normally went into the town every Saturday morning to have a drink at one of their favourite pubs, the Marlborough Arms. It was only a short walk and they would arrive about lunchtime. Howard liked the atmosphere there and he knew Abdul appreciated a place where he was well known.

One day in October, Abdul had some interesting news. "DIASA has offered me the job of Conakry Manager when Pierre Beauregard leaves in January. I've decided to take the job. It will be a chance to do more for the Guinean people than I can do here. I like it here, but the chance of a job in Conakry with all the advantages to help is too good to miss. I feel that educated people, like me, should return."

Howard was amazed how quickly Abdul's English had improved. He paused to digest the news. "We'll miss you and Jeanine. She's been such a good friend to Jean. But an opportunity like this is too good to miss. Definitely take it."

"DIASA says I can come to England when I have my leave, if I like, so we'll keep the house here. They want to use it as a sort of Rest House for visitors to the Banbury office. They'll pay the mortgage and services and we can use it for our visits. Jeanine will stay until Mohamed is old enough to travel out to Guinea. As you know, Guinea can be dangerous for young children."

"Yes. I think you'd make a good manager and this job in Conakry would suit you. Later on I'd like to discuss a business arrangement with you. You could help me set up a branch of our security company in Conakry—a sort of electronic equipment company. There's quite a market in West Africa, as long as you get paid. It wouldn't compromise your position with DIASA and you could have an investment in it if you liked."

"Well, let's wait until I get the job. Would you like another beer? I'm having another cider."

When the drinks arrived, Abdul paid and the men drank them.

"I've just received an interesting piece of news from Banam. A friend of mine saw Suluku the other day and was amazed at how he's changed."

"How do you mean?"

"Well, he's left DIASA and gone into business in Conakry. He now owns a bus and several taxis. There are a lot of rumours flying around that he must have found Buzzard's diamonds. Leila is telling her friends Tom Gough took Buzzard's diamonds to England. But, of course, she can say that now that he's dead."

"I know they weren't found in his luggage because I searched it and sent a list of the contents to his brother in Australia. The brother picked out a few things like photographs and the rest of his things were given to the Salvation Army. David Warner told me to give the silver flask to his sister in Chipping Warden. I phoned her and she collected it from my office."

"I think that flask proves Tom Gough had the diamonds at one time, or at least knew who did. If Leila is correct and he brought them to England, what happened to them? I suppppose he could have swallowed them?"

"Is that possible?"

"Yes. That's what the illegals in Sierra Leone do when the police catch them. We've had cases in Guinea where the gang bosses have cut people open to retrieve diamonds."

"But Tom was cremated. So, if he swallowed any diamonds, they're now at the bottom of the English Channel. Jean emptied his ashes into the sea." Howard paused for a few seconds. "I suppose it's possible Tom gave some to Leila."

"Anything's possible, Howard. You should know that. The only certainty is the possibility of finding diamonds tempt people to behave badly. People can become rich overnight. It's a form of gambling."

Howard hoped Abdul wasn't implying anything. *How many people suspected he had the diamonds.*

"Yes, I think I've done the right thing leaving DIASA. One of the problems out in Guinea was that you couldn't get away from the job. Basically, the company owns you when you're there."

One evening, Howard and Abdul were in the Marlborough Arms in Banbury, having an evening drink. Howard had his usual beer and Abdul was drinking his usual cider. This was their favourite pub.

As they were preparing to leave, Howard saw one of his police friends, sitting at a table by himself.

"Oh, hallo, Ian. I didn't see you sitting there by yourself. You could have joined us. You don't come in here very often these days?"

"No. We've been working on our new house. It's finished now and we're taking a holiday. We've hired a canal boat."

"That sounds interesting. I've always wanted to take a trip on the canal", he paused, "I think you've met Abdul?"

"Yes. We met at the station. I've just had an idea. We have the boat from next Saturday morning, but Susan and Tom won't be back before Monday morning. Her father has been sick and she had to go to see him. He's sicker than we thought and she wants to stay another week. Would you like to help me bring the boat to Banbury? That way we could start from here on Monday morning."

Howard didn't say anything for a few minutes.

"Do you fancy a trip, Abdul?"

"Yes. I've never been on a small boat. It sounds interesting."

"Three's a good number on a boat. Two for the locks and one driving. The boat is near Knowle. I'll arrange for Tom Botham to take us there next Saturday. Okay, if we meet here next Saturday at nine o'clock, I'll arrange supplies and everything."

"Okay. See you next Saturday, then."

As they walked up the road, Howard said, "I hope Jean's not arranged anything for next weekend."

The two wives had not arranged anything for the weekend and seemed pleased their husbands were friendly enough to go on a boat trip together.

CHAPTER 26

O N SATURDAY AT nine o' clock Jeanine drove the two men to the Marlborough Arms to meet Tom Botham and Ian. "Don't fall overboard," she quipped before she drove away.

It took an hour to get to the Grand Union Canal where they were collecting the boat near Knowle. They unloaded the supplies and Tom Botham drove away. "See you in Banbury."

"Thanks for the lift."

Ian spent a few minutes in the office, signing documents. The men went outside to a pond-like area where their boat was tied up with other boats. Their instructor showed them how to start the engine, how to remove any debris or weeds from around the propellor and other simple tasks. "Don't go too fast because the wash destroys the banks of the canal. Just take it steady. I'll meet you at the first lock to show you how to operate it. You're on your own now. Stay on the right side of the canal. Good luck."

Ian Smith decided to steer first. He started the engine and headed out into the canal. It was a mile to the first lock. Just before they arrived, their instructor jumped on board. "This lock goes down and we're lucky because it's full of water. You two jump out and open the gates, so we can drive in."

He stepped onto the stone wall with Abdul and Howard. "Put your back into the beam and push. Notice the foot holds to help with your grip."

Howard found out that it wasn't too difficult to open the gates.

The boat steered up to the second set of gates. Abdul and Howard closed the first set of gates and walked to the second set.

"Now, we have to open the paddles to let the water out so we can go down. That's what these are for," the instructor explained.

He produced two steel tools, bars with sockets at one end, one of which he gave to Howard. "This is how you operate them." He fitted the tool over a squared protrusion and rotated the handle, which lifted the paddles and water flowed into the canal on the lower side. Howard did the same on his set of paddles. Ian steered the boat up to the wooden gates and kept the engine running. The boat went down with the waterr.

"Remember to equalize the water before you open the gates."

When the water was at the lower level, they opened the second set of gates and the barge drove through. Abdul and Howard closed the gates.

"Remember, people can be going down or up, so always close the gates unless someone is following you. You'll get the hang of it." With that, the instructor departed.

"Thanks," Howard said. He and Abdul stepped back on board and the barge floated away.

"Originally, these canals were contructed by hand. You can imagine the amount of work," Ian said.

"Yes. I'm quite impressed," Abdul said.

Howard found that travelling along at a slow speed was very relaxing and, at the same time rather boring. He also found travelling along a waterway and watching the changing scenery was quite interesting. He particularly liked it when they passed through a village and could see people going about their lives.

"This is my kind of speed. How fast are we going?" Abdul asked.

"Oh, three or four miles an hour." Howard, who was steering answered.

"I'm sure that's the problem with modern life. It's too fast. We speed along without looking at anything or anybody."

"I think you have a point, Abdul, this kind of travel shows it. We're combining with nature and people as we go along. Ian, however, thought they were wrong.

"We only get things done quickly, because we can."

Abdul went downstairs to pray at twelve o' clock.

The men changed position every hour and they all took the tiller and steered. The boat was forty feet long, but wasn't too difficult to steer. At one o'clock Ian suggested they stop for lunch.

When they found a suitable mooring place with an iron buoy near a small inn, they tied up the boat and walked along the tow path. The bar only contained six people, sitting on padded seats around the bay windows. The trio walked up to the bar to get themselves drinks and order their lunches. The elderly man behind the bar gave the orders to the cook through a window He seemed interested in Abdul. While he was pouring out the drinks, he spoke to him. "I hope you don't think I'm rude for asking, but do you come from West Africa?'

"Yes. I've just come from Guinea."

"I asked because I used to work in Guinea and Sierra Leone a long time ago."

"Isn't that amazing," Howard exclaimed. "What a coincidence."

"Yes. I used to work for one of the Selection Trust companies before the Second World War."

"Even more amazing. Abdul and I both work in Guinea for another mining company. It's called DIASA. Their headquarters are in Banbury."

"Yes. I left Guinea in 1940 just before the Germans arrived. I knew David Warner and Rory Adams there. Rory was killed in Guinea. He was a good manager and would have done well later on. I didn't like Warner. He only thought of himself." The man paused, as if he realized he had been indiscreet. "Would you care for a drink on the house? Don't worry. I own the pub. Your lunch is ready now."

The men took their free drinks and walked back to their table. After lunch, the men returned to the bar to thank the owner. "Thanks for the drinks."

"Not at all. I enjoyed my time in Guinea and am glad to meet someone from there. What's it like these days?"

"Well, it was bad economically for a few years after the French left. But, it's doing much better now," Abdul said. "This mining company should make things better. We visited the old mine site and saw Rory's grave. Abdul, the clerk, still lives there. Howard now owns Rory's Brough motorcycle."

"It's amazing you found this place today. Talking to you brings back all the old memories. I criticized David Warner because he should have met Rory Adams the night he was killed and didn't. He said he wasn't at the arranged meeting place, and he couldn't wait around. At that time it was terribly dangerous, to stay in the bush alone, especially for someone carrying diamonds. Warner joined the army when he arrived in Sierra Leone. After the war, he made a lot of money, buying and reselling properties. I suppose I was a bit jealous of his success—though I did pretty well in the diamond industry later on and made enough to buy this place."

"Well, we'd better be off now," Ian said. "It's been nice talking to you." Abdul, Ian and Howard shook the owner's hand and the three men went out.

"Wasn't that amazing? In a small place like, this meeting someone who's worked in Guinea?" Howard said.

They walked back to the boat and carried on with their journey. In Warwick, they tied up and walked into the town to have a look at the castle. Afterwards, they journeyed past Leamington Spa and spent the night near Long Itchington. Again, they found a small pub and had dinner.

When they got back to the boat, they had a drink. Ian found a programme on the television he liked and Howard and Abdul discussed the conversation they had had with the inn owner at lunchtime.

"I've heard stories, from some of the old African workers about the murder near Banam. But remember, in those days the managers only told their labourers basic things, mainly commands. The Africans were worried about the arrival of the Vichy French and the loss of their jobs. They knew they were only going to swap one lot of masters for another. Even the war was between European powers. So, the murder was swamped by other news," Abdul said.

"But someone must have realized Warner could have been implicated in the loss of the diamonds?" Howard said.

"If it was Warner, he was lucky. An African was caught going through Mr. Adams clothes. Also a box, with diamonds in it, was retrieved. No one except Mr. Adams knew how many diamonds he was carrying. Everything worked in Warner's favour. My view is that Warner did go back to meet Rory and the pair argued about how many diamonds they would take. Possibly, Warner knocked him out, but must have been disturbed when he was stealing the diamonds and only got away with some of them. Possibly, he took more of them when he went back after the war? You have to remember how chaotic it must have been at that time."

"Yes. You can never tell how people will react in unusual circumstances."

The next morning, the crew was away by eight o' clock because Ian thought they might have a job reaching Banbury by the next morning. They arrived near Wardington, just outside Banbury, before it got dark on Saturday. As they had worked hard, they all went to bed early.

The next morning, they took just over two hours to arrive in Banbury where their wives were waiting.

EPILOGUE

*H*OWARD AND HIS family had been living in Banbury for two years after his return from Guinea when the next major event happened in his life. Abdul and Jeanine returned to Guinea and Howard and his partner, David Rhys worked hard to make their business profitable. Howard bought vehicles for the business and they moved into a bigger building. Howard had not been able to upgrade the condition of the Brough Superior motorcycle.

Jean was pregnant with their second child and they were thinking of buying a bigger house. Jean liked the idea of moving into the old vicarage in Chipping Warden which was again for sale. Howard found the idea of moving into this building bizarre because of its history connecting it to their diamond cache. But, he had agreed to buy it.

It was a nice sunny day when he told David he was going to take the day off.

He went into his garage and wheeled his motorcycle outside. Looking at it, he decided the easiest thing to do was to fix the headlight. It might be something simple like the bulb or a loosewire. Firstly, he removed the rim and reflector and looked inside. By the dusty and grreasy state inside, he could tell it had not been opened for years. He was intrigued to see there were several strips of black insulating tape stuck to the back of the lamp. When these were pried off, he discovered two large diamonds stuck to the back of the tape.

Howard tore the diamonds from the sticky tape. Holding them in the palm of his hand, he looked at them. They looked like two dirty, glassy pebbles. *Who would have thought these baubles would have been responsible for at least two deaths?*